THE BRONTE BOY

A play by

Michael Yates

Nettle Books

The Bronte Boy

Published 2011 by Nettle Books

2nd edition 2017
nettlebooks@hotmail.co.uk
www.nettlebooks.weebly.com

ISBN: 978-0-9933729-4-0

Classification: Drama

Michael Yates has asserted his right under the Copyright, Designs and Patents Act 1988 to be identified as the author of this work. Any company wishing to perform *The Bronte Boy* should contact: michaelyates1066@hotmail.co.uk

Opinions expressed in the play are not necessarily those of the author or publisher.

Cover picture: Warwick St John, Melanie Dagg and Eddie Butler photographed at Haworth Cemetery. Photographer: Lorne Campbell
© 2011, Guzelian Photography, pictures@guzelian.co.uk

The Bronte Boy

The Bronte Boy had its world premiere at the Bradford Playhouse in April 2011. This was part of a tour by the Encore Theatre company in April and May. Other venues were: The Carriageworks theatre in Leeds, The Square Chapel theatre in Halifax, and Wakefield Theatre Royal, venue of the Wakefield Drama Festival.

The Cast:

Branwell..Warwick St John*
Charlotte...Melanie Dagg
John Brown..Eddie Butler
Patrick...Asadour Guzelian
Emily..Vicki Glover**
Anne..Hayley Briggs

Director: Colin Lewisohn
Stage Manager: Peter Meese.   Assistant: Hannah Bachelor

*Warwick St John won the Wakefield Drama Festival
Best Actor award

**Vicki Glover was not available for the Wakefield performance
and her place was taken by Caroline Creagh

In 2013, The Bronte Society sponsored a new production of *The Bronte Boy* for performance at the Society's International AGM weekend. Warwick St John again played Branwell. Director was Marian Mantovani.

Branwell Bronte: how it all went wrong!

I was looking for a nice commercial subject for a play. I wanted to get away from my regular writer's world of politics and adultery set to pop music.

Director Colin Lewisohn had produced a play about Charles Dickens, and someone told him: "You should produce one about JB Priestley." Colin mentioned this as a project that might interest me.

But my wife said: "If you go for a Yorkshire writer, go for the Brontes." And I thought: "If I go for the Brontes, I'll go for Branwell."

Why Branwell? Because he's a failure. I started reading up on him, and I concluded the conventional wisdom was right. He was the alpha male of childhood games, for whom early domination was so easy. Once he grew up and expectation became too much for him, he naturally turned to drink and drugs.

But this sort of abstract psychology won't do for a play, where everything has to be seen, heard and personified. That's where John Brown comes in.

Brown was the parsonage grave-digger and a friend of Branwell, the man who brought Branwell his gin and installed him as a member of the Freemasons. Brown became my villain, someone to twitch upon the dark thread that constantly tugs at Branwell.

I made Brown the kind of insinuating character who knows a bit of maths, a bit of science, a bit of the Bible, and who welds these into a deadly philosophy, turning love of the common man into worship of mediocrity. Where my Brontes talk in a pastiche of literary language, my Brown talks like a street-corner politician. He is charming, comic, sinister. If the real Brown were alive today, he could sue me for libel and take my house.

And I played around with the time scheme. In reality, Branwell became a Mason at an early age; for the sake of the drama, his initiation comes at the end of my play and happens at Christmas, while the other Brontes are staying home and celebrating.

If you saw the play on its tour of Yorkshire, you'll notice I've made a few changes.

I discovered after the run that the tune to *Abide With Me*, featured in our version of Charlotte's funeral, wasn't written until six years after her death. Ouch. I have now substituted *O God Our Help in Ages Past*.

As John Brown says in Act II: *Writers! What do they know?*

And he's dead right.

Michael Yates

CHARACTERS (in order of appearance)

Branwell Bronte
Patrick Bronte, parish curate, Branwell's father
Charlotte Bronte, Branwell's older sister
Emily Bronte, Branwell's younger sister
Anne Bronte, Branwell's younger sister
John Brown, parish sexton
Coachman (disembodied voice)
Tavern landlord (disembodied voice)

The play is set in the first half of the 19th century, mainly in and around the family home at Haworth, Yorkshire, and in a London Tavern and a Masonic Hall.

Length: Two Hours

Furnishings: desk, table, three wooden chairs

Props: Table cloth; wooden hobby horse; besom-style broom; quill pen; ink well; small exercise book; glass decanter; pewter jug; three spirit glasses; four wine glasses; three framed pictures, only seen from behind; a dozen toy soldiers and other figures in a wooden box; various papers, letters and envelopes; clay pipe; shovel; walking stick; two fat paperback books covered in brown paper; a Medieval sword; small leather-bound Bible; large hardback book decorated with occult symbols; wine bottle; fruit juice; white scarf used as blindfold.

Recorded music: Chopin, Ballades, op 23 and 38; Strauss, The Radetsky March; Mozart, Concerto for Bassoon and Orchestra, Overture from The Magic Flute; Hymns: To Be a Pilgrim, O God Our Help in Ages Past.

Sound effects: Stagecoach sounds including driver's shouts; crowd sounds for tavern; bird song for outdoors; a woman's sobbing; a woman's scream

ACT I, SCENE 1.

WE HEAR CHOPIN'S BALLADE II FOR PIANO, OPUS 38. AS IT FADES, SPOTLIGHTS COME ON REVEALING ELDERLY PATRICK STAGE RIGHT, 30-YEAR-OLD BRANWELL STAGE LEFT. THEY WALK TOWARDS EACH OTHER, SPOTLIGHTS FOLLOWING. BRANWELL IS WEARING A CRUMPLED DRESSING GOWN, HIS EYES ARE BLEARY AND HE STUMBLES AND APPEARS ONLY HALF AWAKE. PATRICK IS DRESSED IN CLERICAL GARB AND EXUDES DIGNITY.

PATRICK: (SHOUTING) Hear me! You will *hear* me, sir!

BRANWELL: (SHOUTING) I *hear* you, sir! I *hear* you!

PATRICK: (SHOUTING) You do *not*, sir! You do not listen!

BRANWELL: (SUDDENLY QUIETER) I listen sir! I listen, father! (BEAT) Oh father... (RAISES HIS HANDS BRIEFLY IN GESTURE OF PRAYER)

PATRICK: (SHOUTING) It is noon, sir! Noon! And you are not yet dressed!

BRANWELL: (SHOUTING) I *am* dressed, sir! I am dressed well enough. (BEAT, THEN MORE QUIETLY) For the house, sir. For my study. Well enough for the house.

PATRICK: (HESITATING) I would help you dress if...

BRANWELL: (ANGRY) Sir, I am your son but I am no longer your child!

PATRICK: (SHOUTING) You are in drink, sir! Look at you!

BRANWELL: (SHOUTING) I have had a *glass*, father. That is all. (MORE QUIETLY) And I have looked in that glass. I have seen my face, sir. I know my face!

PATRICK: (SHOUTING) There is work to be done. (MORE QUIETLY) There is always work.

BRANWELL: (SHOUTING) I *do* my work, father. I work. (BEAT) Even now, I return to it. I return to my desk.

PATRICK: (MORE QUIETLY) Well then, I shall be pleased to see it. When it is finished. Whatever your work may be. (HE EXITS STAGE LEFT)

BRANWELL: (MORE QUIETLY) Finished. (BEAT) Father. (BEAT) Our father... (BEAT) Father, I go to my desk. I go to my work. I go now!

SPOTLIGHTS OFF

ACT I, SCENE 2.

LIGHTS GO UP ON DESK AND CHAIR STAGE RIGHT. THERE IS A PILE OF PAPERS ON THE DESK TOGETHER WITH A GLASS DECANTER, A SMALL GLASS BOTTLE, A QUILL PEN AND INK WELL AND A SPIRIT GLASS. THREE FRAMED PAINTINGS LEAN AGAINST THE DESK THOUGH WE CANNOT SEE THE FRONTS OF THEM. BRANWELL WALKS OVER TO THE DESK AND SITS ON CHAIR BEHIND IT. SLOWLY, AFTER SIFTING THE PAPERS, HE PICKS ONE UP

BRANWELL: (READING) To the editor, Blackwoods
Magazine. (BEAT) Sir, read what I write. If it please
you. Read what I have *written*. Write. Written. *Have*
written. (BEAT) Yes. (HE BEGINS CROSSING
OUT AND RE-WRITING. HE READS IT BACK)
Sir, read what I have written. If it please you. I have
addressed you twice before and now I do so yet again.
(GLANCES UP) Oh, let it please you. Oh God, oh
Father, let it please the editor.(CONTINUES TO
READ) I have attached a poem of my own devising,
which the editor of the Halifax Guardian has seen fit
to print this last month. The Halifax Guardian is a
most learned and respectable newspaper within the
county of Yorkshire. (STOPS, PONDERS) But what
will they think now it is already published? Will they
think it used and stale? (WRITES) I trust, sir, that you
will not think it used and stale that it has already been
published, for the Halifax Guardian is seldom read
beyond the bounds of Halifax itself. (BEAT) No, no!
(HE DROPS THE PAPER BACK ON THE DESK)
We shall start again, Mr Editor. A new paragraph, a
new sentence, sir. (HE GLANCES AT THE
DECANTER, STRETCHES OUT A HAND AND
TOUCHES IT) That I might drink and leave the
world unseen, Mr Keats. (CATCHES HIMSELF) The
Royal Academy. I had already begun a new epistle.

HE SEARCHES FOR THE ACADEMY LETTER

BRANWELL: Oh where..? Where..? Ah! (HE PICKS UP
NEW SHEET) Yes, yes. (HE READS) The Secretary,
The Royal Academy. (BEAT) Sir, you will recall this
is not the first time I have written to you. (THINKS
ALOUD) *Have* written. Wrote. No. *Have* written!
(CROSSES OUT, WRITES, READS ON) We had
arranged an appointment and I was to bring you some

of my paintings, half a dozen small watercolours which I consider bear comparison with the early works of Mr Turner, and which my friends, all learned men hereabout, had said were not without merit. (HE BECOMES AGITATED) I also planned to bring two larger oil paintings which my friends and family had also enjoyed and over which the name of Mr Gainsborough was frequently invoked. By so doing, I had been hoping to forego some of the formal examination procedure which is customary with you.

HE STOPS, PUTS PAPER DOWN ON DESK, RESTS HIS HEAD IN HIS HANDS, LIFTS ONE OF THE CANVASES AND STUDIES IT BRIEFLY, THEN DROPS IT BACK ON THE FLOOR. HE PICKS UP THE PAPER AGAIN

BRANWELL: (READING) But alas, when the scheduled day came, I was, I regret to say, inconvenienced (BEAT) No, no. *Obstructed.* (HE CROSSES OUT, WRITES) Obstructed by some family business which was wholly unforeseen. I trust, sir that you will allow me to make amends, even at this late hour, by admitting me to a further appointment. (BEAT) I am still able to bring you the oil paintings which, by happy coincidence, are still unsold despite my having begun a thriving portraiture establishment in Bradford. The paintings are first, of my sisters, of which I have three remaining. (GLANCES UP) That is, three *sisters.* (BEAT) But also three *paintings.* (GLANCES AWAY) To tell truth, I have very many paintings remaining. (READS) And second I can bring you a depiction of the countryside near Haworth rectory which is our home. (STOPS READING) I tried to do one of *you,* father, but I couldn't catch the likeness.

HE REACHES OUT TO THE DECANTER AND FILLS A
GLASS.

BRANWELL: (PICKING UP NEW SHEET OF PAPER)
Now. What is this? (READS) To the Directors, the
Leeds and Manchester Railroad. Dear Sirs, I write to
bring to your attention a very grave injustice.(BEAT)
Some years ago, I served as an employee of your
company at the Sowerby Bridge Railway station.
During my term of duty, a sum of money…

HE PAUSES, SCRUNCHES UP THE PAPER AND DROPS
IT ON THE DESK. HE FINDS ANOTHER PIECE OF
PAPER AND BEGINS TO WRITE HURRIEDLY.

BRANWELL: (READING AS HE WRITES) John Brown,
Sexton of the Parish. (BEAT) Friend John, My spirits
are low. I shall feel very much obliged if you can
contrive to bring me five pence worth of gin in a
proper measure. I could perhaps take it from you at
the lane top when I shall imburse you. I shall get this
letter to you in the usual way…

HE DRAINS HIS GLASS, PUTS IT DOWN AND BEGINS
TO SLUMP. AS HE DOES SO, CHARLOTTE ENTERS
SLOWLY STAGE LEFT AND STANDS SOME WAY
BEHIND BRANWELL. SHE IS WEARING A GREY
CLOAK AND HOOD. SHE STANDS PERFECTLY STILL
LIKE A GHOST, UNSEEN BY HIM. HE MEANWHILE
POURS A GLASS OF GIN AND BEGINS TO SIP IT.

BRANWELL: (AT MENTION OF EACH OF THE NAMES
HE RAISES HIS GLASS WITH BRAVADO AND
TAKES A FURTHER SIP) One glass. That's all I've
had today, Mr Editor, Mr Secretary, Mr

Gainsborough, Mr Railway Director... (VOICE
RISES) Mr Reverend Bronte!

AT THE LAST NAME HE DRAINS THE GLASS. WHEN
HE HAS DONE SO, HE LOOKS AT IT SURPRISED AND
PUTS IT DOWN

BRANWELL: And a draught or two of laudanum. (HE SIPS
FROM THE SMALL GLASS BOTTLE) Well, I have
a cold. It's good for me. Emily takes it regularly.
Charlotte used to. And that friend of hers. That
Gaskell woman. Takes it all the time. Only thing is: it
does make you sleepy. It makes you dream.

HE MOANS, HOLDS HIS HEAD IN HIS HANDS, THEN
SLUMPS FORWARD, RESTS HIS HEAD ON THE DESK
AND FALLS ASLEEP.

ACT I, SCENE 3.

LIGHTS COME UP STAGE LEFT, REVEALING A TABLE
COVERED IN CLOTH ON WHICH IS A WOODEN TOY
FORT AND VARIOUS SMALL FIGURES – SOLDIERS,
ZULUS ETC. CHARLOTTE THROWS OFF HER CLOAK
AND HOOD AND IS REVEALED IN A DRESS WITH A
CHILD'S FRILLY APRON. IN THE FOLLOWING
DIALOGUE, CHARLOTTE AND BRANWELL ARE
CHILDREN OF NO SPECIFIC AGE. THEY SKIP ABOUT
AND SPEAK IN DELIBERATELY CHILDISH TONES
WHILE USING ADULT VOCABULARY.

CHARLOTTE: (PUMMELLING HIM) Brother, brother, be
awake!

BRANWELL: (DROWSY) What?

CHARLOTTE: I want to play! I want to play!

CHARLOTTE RUNS BACK BEHIND THE TABLE STAGE LEFT, PICKS UP THE HOBBY HORSE AND RIDES IT ROUND THE STAGE. BRANWELL SMILES, LEAPS TO HIS FEET, STRIPS OFF HIS DRESSING GOWN TO REVEAL A SOLDIER'S TUNIC. HE CHASES AFTER HER AND HUGS HER.

BRANWELL: Charlotte! Yes, I'll play. But not *girls'* games! Not games that *girls* play!

CHARLOTTE: (PEEVED) *I* don't play girls' games!

BRANWELL: (THINKS) No, you don't! (BEAT) Allright then! We'll play (BEAT) *war*!

CHARLOTTE: (CLAPS HER HANDS) La guerre!

BRANWELL: Is that French? I do not like French.

CHARLOTTE: You do not like French because you do not know any.

BRANWELL: I do not care to learn it. It is not a *man's* language. Not like English. I think it is the lack of consonants that spoils it for a man.

CHARLOTTE: I *love* French. But then, I suppose I *am* a girl.

BRANWELL: But you like war!

CHARLOTTE: Oh yes! I do! We'll have battles and massacres and carnage! I *love* carnage!

BRANWELL: I am glad. For I do tend to *write* carnage. When I am in the mood.

HE RIFLES ONE OF THE DESK DRAWERS, REMOVES A TINY EXERCISE BOOK

13

BRANWELL: Look. (OPENING THE BOOK) It is all here.
I have worked very hard on it. I trust you will find as
much carnage as your heart may desire.

CHARLOTTE: Oh, I'm sure I shall. (BEAT) What is the
story? (SHE DROPS THE HOBBY HORSE AND
RUNS ACROSS TO HIM)

BRANWELL: (THUMBS THROUGH EXERCISE BOOK)
This is a great day for the Glasstown Confederacy.

CHARLOTTE: (CLAPS HER HANDS AND SKIPS) Oh yes!
Oh yes! (CATCHING HERSELF) Why?

BRANWELL: Because they are poised to conquer the whole
of the nation of Angria in the name of King Zamorna
and raise their banner among the African natives, of
course. And when they have done so, why! There will
be other lands and other worlds to conquer. For
Angria, once a backward and pagan state, shall take
its rightful place among the powerful nations of the
earth.

CHARLOTTE: Bravo! (BEAT) And is there *love* in the
story?

BRANWELL: Love? Why should there be love?

CHARLOTTE: There is always love. Otherwise (SHE
LOOKS EMBARRASSED) what will the soldiers do
when they have won? They must have something to
do when the battle is won.

BRANWELL: (THINKS) Well, I suppose they will
celebrate.

CHARLOTTE: How?

BRANWELL: With feasts. As you find in Mr Shakespeare. In Macbeth, for example.

CHARLOTTE: And dancing? Will there be dancing? As you find in Miss Austen?

BRANWELL: (SHOCKED) You are reading Miss Austen?

CHARLOTTE: (SUDDENLY DEFENSIVE) Only when I am tired. Or I have a headache.

BRANWELL: It would require a very *large* headache to induce *me* to read Miss Austen. Why, there are no massacres, no carnage...

CHARLOTTE: It is true I *do* enjoy carnage, but in its proper place. (PAUSE) Well...(BEAT) Where are the English soldiers?

BRANWELL: You know where the English soldiers are. In their box. Where they always are.

CHARLOTTE: Then you must let them out! You're good at letting out the soldiers.

BRANWELL PUTS DOWN THE EXERCISE BOOK, TAKES A WOODEN BOX FROM A DESK DRAWER AND FROM THE BOX TAKES TWO OR THREE TOY SOLDIERS

CHARLOTTE: (POINTING) That young one there is very handsome!

BRANWELL: It is his uniform makes him so. (BEAT) Sometimes I think we should all wear uniforms. Everyone should be known for what he is – a colonel, a lieutenant, a private.

CHARLOTTE: And for what *she* is.

BRANWELL: Don't be silly. You don't have girls in the army.

CHARLOTTE: I'm sure you do. I read somewhere about some women who were (BEAT) camp followers.

BRANWELL: Well, it was probably like the song when Sweet Polly Oliver followed her sweetheart to the wars. But she only *dressed* as a soldier. She wasn't really one of them.

CHARLOTTE: But it's the uniform that matters. That's what *you* said.

BRANWELL: Except when it comes to girls.

CHARLOTTE: That one there. (POINTS) He looks a bit like father.

BRANWELL: Right. He can be the general. General Percy.

CHARLOTTE: But he's not got a general's uniform.

BRANWELL: If he's father, then he'll be the general.

CHARLOTTE: But that's not what you said… (GIVES IN) Oh. Allright.

THEY CARRY THE BOX OF SOLDIERS UPSTAGE LEFT AND SPILL THEM OUT ON TO THE TABLE

BRANWELL: The redoubtable General Percy is very important. For when King Zamorna has gained his victories, I think General Percy will plot against him. I think they may be rivals for domination.

HE STUDIES THE TABLE TOP

BRANWELL: Where is the artillery? Where are the big guns?

CHARLOTTE: Dear brother, do not take this amiss but... (PAUSE) You said *poised*. Poised to conquer. That's what you said. Sometimes it is not enough to be *poised*. (BEAT) Perhaps something untoward will happen…

BRANWELL: Something untoward? Never.

CHARLOTTE: Perhaps.

BRANWELL: No. Never. They have proved their mettle, they have proved their…

CHARLOTTE: Their steel.

BRANWELL: (ANNOYED) No, Charlotte. When I say they have proved their *mettle,* I spell it differently. It is the word mettle meaning courage and ardent temperament, not the word metal meaning an elementary substance such as gold or iron or tin.

CHARLOTTE: (ADORING) You are so *clever*, Branwell. You are so grown-up. You sometimes make me forget I am the elder by a good twelve-month.

BRANWELL: It is because I am a boy. Boys have larger brains. (BEAT) Well, if we can't find the artillery it will have to be hand-to-hand.

HE ATTACKS THE ZULUS BY SMASHING THEM WITH ONE OR TWO ENGLISH SOLDIERS WHILE MAKING EXPLOSIVE NOISES IN THE BACK OF HIS THROAT

CHARLOTTE: (HOLDS OUT HER HAND) Let *me* have father!

BRANWELL: Why?

CHARLOTTE: Hand-to-hand is extremely taxing on the constitution. And he is a person of sedentary pursuits, unused to the African climate.

BRANWELL: He is a *man*! And hand-to-hand is no sacrifice for such as he, who has risen to the rank of general.

CHARLOTTE: I do not want him to be a casualty. I do not want him to partake of the carnage. I do not want him to die or be in any way posthumous!

THERE IS A SUDDEN SILENCE. BRANWELL STOPS SMASHING THE ZULUS. BOTH LOOK DOWN AT THE FLOOR. EVENTUALLY…

BRANWELL: He will not die. Has he not proved himself? Has he not outlived so many others in this war?

CHARLOTTE: Maria.

BRANWELL: Elizabeth.

CHARLOTTE: Our sisters.

BRANWELL: And our mother.

CHARLOTTE: Our household…

BRANWELL: (REPEATS) Household… (BEAT) cavalry. Why do we have so few cavalry?

BRANWELL RESUMES HIS SMASHING OF THE ZULUS. THEN…

BRANWELL: Look. Perhaps he will be *wounded*. General Percy will be wounded. Wounded *only*!

CHARLOTTE: (HORRIFIED) Oh no!

BRANWELL: (QUICKLY) He will not die.

CHARLOTTE: He *must* not!

BRANWELL: *You* will nurse him back to health.

CHARLOTTE: (SUSPICIOUS) Will he be wounded for long?

BRANWELL: Not if you nurse him well. Not if we choose it differently.

CHARLOTTE: Then let us choose it differently. (BEAT) I would not want to spend my *life* nursing father.

A BRIEF SILENCE

BRANWELL: (CONCEDING) You know, perhaps there *might* be dancing. A ball perhaps. If the officers wished.

CHARLOTTE: It will be a chance for the officers to while away their time during the peace.

BRANWELL: There will not be peace for long. It is not the way of things.

CHARLOTTE: It can be for a *short* time. A ball does not take up more than a *short* time. It is a necessary thing that officers should meet young ladies. And the king of Angria should meet them too.

BRANWELL: Why the king? Why King Zamorna, the great warrior of Angria?

CHARLOTTE: Why, kings even more than officers. For kings must have sons to occupy their thrones after them.

BRANWELL: (GRUDGINGLY) Very well. Then Zamorna, the mighty warrior of Angria, shall marry. (BEAT) He shall marry Mary, the daughter of General Percy.

CHARLOTTE: But King Zamorna and General Percy do not seem well-matched. You said yourself they are secret rivals in the struggle for domination.

BRANWELL: That is what I am writing in my History of Angria.

CHARLOTTE: Of course, if King Zamorna and Miss Percy love each other truly, then no-one should stand in their way.

BRANWELL: General Percy will see that this is his chance of winning favour with Zamorna. And Zamorna will see that it is *his* way of controlling General Percy. He will make General Percy his Prime Minister.

CHARLOTTE: And will that lead to another war?

BRANWELL: Of course.

CHARLOTTE: Even though they are become the same family?

BRANWELL: It is always so with great families that they should wage war and kill each other. Consider. Richard III and the Duke of Clarence were brothers.

(BEAT) I must write this down. (HE RUSHES
BACK TO THE DESK AND PICKS UP THE PEN)

CHARLOTTE: I am grown bored with this. I do not want the
family to kill each other.

BRANWELL: It is only what you get in Sir Walter Scott.
The Highland Clans. I thought you *liked* Sir Walter.

CHARLOTTE: I am now less for Sir Walter and more for
Lord Byron.

BRANWELL: You told me you *adored* Sir Walter. Sir
Walter is a man who knows his battles and his
soldiery. Why should you change? What faults do you
now perceive in Sir Walter?

CHARLOTTE: Perhaps he is too (BEAT) Scotch. (PAUSE) I
do not know. About Lord Byron, there is something,
well, I cannot say what something, but it is not at all
Scotch.

BRANWELL: And yet I believe there is some Scotchness
about him…

CHARLOTTE: Then he has hid it well.

ANOTHER BRIEF SILENCE THEN…

CHARLOTTE: Will General Percy really go to war against
King Zamorna?

BRANWELL: It is inevitable.

CHARLOTTE: But they have so much in common. A woman
who loves them both…

BRANWELL: It is destiny. For a woman, love is destiny.
For a man...

CHARLOTTE: What is it for a man?

BRANWELL: To be something in the world. To be...
(BEAT) A girl would not understand it.

CHARLOTTE: I think perhaps I do. I think perhaps it is
found somewhat in Byron.

PATRICK: (DISEMBODIED VOICE) Children!
Children! Where are you?

CHARLOTTE: Father! It's father! Quick, put the soldiers
away. Keep them safe.

BRANWELL: (SCORNFUL) You cannot keep soldiers *safe*.
It is not their nature.

THE CHILDREN PUT THE BOX OF SOLDIERS AND
THE EXERCISE BOOK BACK IN THE DESK DRAWERS.
CHARLOTTE SMOOTHES HER APRON AND
BRANWELL PULLS HIS SOLDIER'S TUNIC DOWN
ABOUT HIM. THEY LOOK LIKE A PAIR OF
CLANDESTINE LOVERS REMOVING THE EVIDENCE
OF THEIR ENCOUNTER. THEN...

BRANWELL: Come. Let us speak with our father.

CHARLOTTE: With the redoubtable General Percy.

BRANWELL PICKS UP HIS DRESSING GOWN AND
SLINGS IT ACROSS HIS SHOULDER. CHARLOTTE
PICKS UP THE HOBBY HORSE AND MOUNTS IT.
THEY RUN OFF UPSTAGE RIGHT. AS THEY DO SO,

WE HEAR THE CHORUS OF THE RADETSKY MARCH
BY JOHANN STRAUSS. LIGHTS DIM.

ACT I, SCENE 4.

LIGHTS GO UP. ENTER PATRICK UPSTAGE RIGHT, IN
CLERICAL GARB

PATRICK: (HOLDING A LETTER AND SHOUTING)
               Children! Children! Where are you? Branwell!
               Charlotte! Emily! Anne! Come to me! Come! Here!

SUPREMELY CONFIDENT, HE WAITS IN SMILING
SILENCE AS THEY SLOWLY ASSEMBLE FROM ALL
POINTS. BRANWELL AND CHARLOTTE ARE NOW,
LIKE THE REST, DRESSED AS ADULTS, BRANWELL
IN WAISTCOAT AND TROUSERS, CHARLOTTE IN THE
SAME DRESS BUT WITHOUT THE CHILD'S APRON.
EMILY CARRIES A BROOM AND WEARS A HEAD
SCARF SO SHE HAS OBVIOUSLY BEEN DOING
HOUSEWORK. THERE IS A CONFUSION OF
INQUISITIVE VOICES. HAVING MILKED THE DRAMA
FOR ALL IT IS WORTH, PATRICK CLAPS HIS HANDS
AND THERE IS SUDDEN SILENCE

PATRICK: Work! There is always work! But always the
               works of the Almighty are great and good! And today,
               under his guidance, our own work has come to
               fruition! I have here a letter (HE WAVES IT
               ABOUT) from (PAUSE) The Royal Academy!

SHARP INTAKE OF BREATH FROM THE OTHERS,
THEN RAGGED CHEERS

PATRICK: Branwell, I have taken the liberty of opening
               this missive, though it is clearly addressed to you.

BRANWELL: I forgive you, father.

HE PUTS OUT HIS HAND TO TAKE IT BUT PATRICK
PULLS THE LETTER AWAY

PATRICK: (CLEARLY ENJOYING HIMSELF)
                Branwell has been offered an interview with the
                Royal Academy for a place among their students. He
                is to meet with the secretary on the second of next
                month. *All their works they do to be seen of men.*
                Matthew 23.

WITH A FLOURISH HE HANDS THE LETTER TO
BRANWELL

BRANWELL: (HE TAKES HIS TIME READING IT,
                THEN) There is still an examination, father, a
                procedure to be followed, before I can be taught there.

PATRICK: (GAZING AT BRANWELL) But for one like
                yourself, my son, I fully expect it will be waived. You
                have much to show them...

BRANWELL: (NERVOUSLY) I have a few paintings of
                some worth...

ANNE: (INTERRUPTING) Oh they are brilliant! *You*
                are brilliant, Branwell!

PATRICK: (GAZING AT BRANWELL) Thank you,
                Anne!

EMILY: He will be *such* a success, will he not, father?

PATRICK: (GAZING AT BRANWELL) I believe he
                will, Emily. He has been well taught, I know, by my
                friend Mr Williams in his studio in Leeds.

BRANWELL: And I have tried, sir, to copy from nature.

CHARLOTTE: We have *all of us* tried to copy from nature, father. We have *all*, I believe, reached a certain dexterity with the sketching pencil.

PATRICK: (FINALLY LOOKS AWAY FROM BRANWELL) Dexterity. (BEAT) It is no more than I should expect of my family, Charlotte. *Everyman's work shall be made manifest.* Corinthians Chapter 3.

CHARLOTTE: And every *woman's*?

PATRICK: (GAZING AT BRANWELL AGAIN) My children are olive branches round my table but there is one will grow like a cedar in Lebanon.

EMILY: (INTERRUPTING) But supposing he falls?

PATRICK: (ANNOYED) He does not fall, Emily.

ANNE: He *used* to fall, father. All the time.

PATRICK: That was many years ago, Anne. And it was *not* all the time. It was (BEAT) a thing of childhood. It was grown out of.

CHARLOTTE: If it is the second of the month, father, when Branwell must go forth…

PATRICK: …to the Royal Academy! (HE TURNS TO CHARLOTTE) Yes?

CHARLOTTE: Father, there are great preparations to be made. And precious little time.

PATRICK: Yes, yes. Breeches to be washed, bread to be baked, pictures to be framed, tickets to be bought…

(BEAT) I rely on you to organise the details, Charlotte. And I say to the rest of my family: Do as Charlotte tells you. It is a great adventure for all of us and we must all play our part.

HE PUTS HIS HANDS ON BRANWELL'S SHOULDERS. LIGHTS DIM. SPOTLIGHT COMES UP ON BRANWELL AND PATRICK

BRANWELL: (TIMIDLY) A few paintings of some worth.

PATRICK: *For to be seen of men.*

BRANWELL: And I have tried, sir, to copy from nature.

PATRICK: *And your work made manifest.*

CHARLOTTE: (DISEMBODIED VOICE) And precious little *time*!

SPOTLIGHTS OFF. STAGE IN DARKNESS. THEN…

ACT I, SCENE 5.

LIGHTS UP. THE NEXT SECTION COMPRISES TWO SEPARATE SCENES VIEWED SIMULTANEOUSLY, AND THE CHARACTERS IN EACH TAKE TURNS TO SPEAK. STAGE RIGHT IS FURNISHED AS BEFORE. CHARLOTTE IS SEATED AT DESK WITH OPEN SCRAPBOOK, EMILY IS STANDING, ANNE SITTING ON DESKTOP, ALL OF THEM FROZEN IN TIME. AT STAGE LEFT, THE CLOTH HAS BEEN REMOVED FROM THE TABLE ALONG WITH THE TOYS, AND TWO CHAIRS HAVE BEEN ADDED, ONE EACH SIDE. A MAN IN A TOP HAT AND OVERCOAT IS SEATED SIDE

OF TABLE STAGE LEFT. HIS ATTITUDE IS
DOWNCAST AND HIS FACE IS HIDDEN. A JUG AND
TWO UPTURNED GLASSES LIE ON THE TABLE.
SOUND OF COACH AND HORSES ARRIVING.
WHENEVER THE SCENE MOVES STAGE LEFT, THERE
IS BACKGROUND NOISE OF THE TAVERN CROWD

COACHMAN: (DISEMBODIED VOICE) Whoaa!!! Whoa
    there!

BRANWELL: (DISEMBODIED VOICE) A room. One
    night only. A room and a fire and a meal and…

LANDLORD: (DISEMBODIED VOICE) And a jug of
    something, sir? Spirits?

BRANWELL: (DISEMBODIED VOICE) No, I am already
    in *good* spirits.

BRANWELL ENTERS WEARING OVERCOAT STAGE
LEFT. HE LOOKS ROUND BRIEFLY. AFTER SLIGHT
HESITATION, HE GOES TO TABLE AND SITS
OPPOSITE MAN IN HAT. HE DRUMS HIS FINGERS ON
THE TABLE AND GAZES ROUND. ACTORS STAGE
LEFT FREEZE.

CHARLOTTE: (HOLDING TINY EXERCISE BOOK)
    General Percy will *not* die. When King Zamorna has
    gained his victories, I think General Percy will plot
    against him. I think they may be rivals for
    domination. But I think neither of them need die.

ANNE: (LYING LANGUOROUSLY ACROSS
    DESK TOP) I do not *care* if they live or die.

SHE GIGGLES AND LEAPS TO HER FEET

CHARLOTTE: (SHOCKED) Anne! How can you...?

ANNE: (WANTING TO ANNOY) They are not *real*, sister! They are only (BEAT) stories.

CHARLOTTE: (ANGRY) There was a time when you respected King Zamorna and General Percy, when you more readily took part in the great and chivalrous deeds of Angria!

CHARLOTTE THROWS THE EXERCISE BOOK DOWN ON THE DESK

EMILY: There are other lands and other worlds to explore, Charlotte. Now Anne and I have become pilgrims.

ANNE: Yes. Pilgrims.

EMILY: We have decided to traverse further afield. We have our own country now (BEAT) where the people *listen* to us.

CHARACTERS STAGE RIGHT FREEZE. STAGE LEFT, JOHN BROWN, THE STRANGER IN THE TOP HAT, REMOVES IT AND GLANCES ACROSS AT BRANWELL

BROWN: Why, Mr Branwell sir! Of all the folk...

BRANWELL: (SURPRISED) I do not... (BEAT) Why, it is Brown, is it not? John Brown?

BROWN: It is, Mr Branwell. John Brown. Tha father's sexton. (LAUGHS) Tha father's gravedigger.

BRANWELL: (LAUGHS AWKWARDLY) I cannot conceive it! That I should arrive at this very inn in the great metropolis and discover you here!

BROWN: The coach road from Bradford to London is well travelled, sir. If we have made that same journey, even at differing times, it is no surprise we should meet here. What, if I may ask, brings thee to this destination?

BRANWELL: (RETICENT) Why, I hope, Brown, that it may be not so much my destination but a mere staging post, if I may use that metaphor...

BROWN: Why, you may, sir. Of course you may. What is a metaphor to a gentleman like yourself? I myself am *happy* with a metaphor. For we are all readers now, sir. We working folk too have our schoolhouses and our libraries.

BRANWELL: Yes! It is a great age we live in. (BEAT) I am a sort of pilgrim, Brown, and my quest is to stake my claim to be a part of this great age. I have an interview with the Royal Academy. Tomorrow morning, nine o'clock sharp.

BROWN: And I'm sure that's what tha'll be, sir. Sharp as a butcher's knife. (BEAT) But I too am a pilgrim.

JOHN BROWN LOOKS ROUND AS THOUGH FEARING EAVESDROPPERS

BRANWELL: (HOOKED) And what is your quest?

BROWN: Nothing less than the sacred work of the Great Architect of the Universe.

BRANWELL: You mean God?

BROWN: That is not a name I speak lightly, sir. But ay, I do mean God. Here. Let me pour a libation.

HE TURNS OVER THE GLASSES AND PICKS UP THE JUG. CHARACTERS STAGE LEFT FREEZE.

CHARLOTTE: I do not know what quest you can pursue in another country, sisters, that you cannot pursue in the perfectly adequate nation founded by Branwell and myself. You should not speak lightly of Angria. Your brother and I have constructed our nation with painstaking detail, that there should be for all of us a land of justice and nobility, a land of…

EMILY: Cannon!

ANNE: And war!

EMILY: And parades!

ANNE: And politics! (BEAT) Ugh!

CHARLOTTE: These are the very things of life. What else can there be?

ANNE: Poetry. There is no poetry in Angria. Only battle hymns. And speeches. For when people die.

EMILY: So we two have founded an entirely new country. Gondal.

CHARLOTTE: (ANGRY NOW) And what would I find in Gondal? If I should care to make such an excursion in the first place? Which I very much doubt I should.

ANNE: (WAVING HER ARMS) Joy! Ecstasy!

EMILY: (INTERRUPTING) Not *all* the time, it has to be said. For I think it is not wholly proper to require joy and ecstasy *all* the time. (BEAT) But now and again. That is perfectly acceptable. With perhaps a little pain intermingled. (DECLAIMS) Darkness and glory rejoicingly blending/ earth rising to heaven and heaven descending/ man's spirit away from its drear dungeon sending...

SHE PIROUETTES AND GAZES INSOLENTLY AT CHARLOTTE. ANNE BURSTS OUT LAUGHING.

ANNE: (TO EMILY) It is good! (TO CHARLOTTE) Is it not good, Emily's poem?

CHARLOTTE: Why, yes! (BEAT) It is *promising.*

EMILY: (TEASING CHARLOTTE) Only promising?

CHARLOTTE: (DEFENSIVE) More than promising perhaps. But the mood is uncertain. How can darkness and glory rejoicingly blend? No, no. I consider it too metaphysical. And the mood changes are too abrupt. Drear dungeon, indeed!

EMILY STALKS CHARLOTTE IN SLOW MOTION LIKE A JUNGLE CAT AND ENDS WITH HER FACE VERY CLOSE TO HER SISTER'S

EMILY: (EXAGGERATED IMITATION OF CHARLOTTE) *Drear dungeon indeed*! (BEAT) But if Branwell had written it...

ANNE: If Branwell had spoken it...

EMILY: Why, then it would be light as birdsong...

SHE POSES WITH ARMS ABOVE HER HEAD

ANNE: And we should be carried away on the wings of poesy!

SHE WAVES HER ARMS LIKE WINGS

CHARLOTTE: (VERY ANGRY NOW) Do not speak slightingly of your brother! You would not do so if he were here.

EMILY: And where is he?

CHARLOTTE: You know only too well...

EMILY: Tell us again!

ANNE: For we are only children and we are forgetful!

CHARLOTTE: Why, Branwell is making his way in the world as we shall all need to do.

EMILY: Away from this dreary dungeon!

CHARLOTTE: If you care to think of it as such!

THEY FREEZE. JOHN BROWN POURS THE GIN STAGE LEFT...

BROWN: Free, Mr Branwell. All men free from the dungeon of life. Free to live as brothers. Free to do owt they please if it please the Architect.

BRANWELL: Brotherly love? Is that not the teaching of our own Lord Jesus?

BROWN: It is, ay. And we Masons do not deny the Lord Jesus. Nor the Hebrew Lord of Moses. Nor the

Lord of the Mohammedans. Nor any Lord. (PAUSE) But we are, sir, more practical. For that is the nature of God, is it not? He has designed and structured a universe more powerful than the steam engine, more beautiful than the blast furnace, more teeming with life than the backstreets of Manchester, a universe of infinite beauty! And what does he ask of us?

BRANWELL: What? (HE TAKES A DRINK)

BROWN: Only that we acknowledge the three great needs of man. First, that we honour and respect each other, every degree and kind and appetite. (BEAT) Though of course, I do not include Papists.

BRANWELL: (SHOCKED) Why, no!

BROWN: Second, that we relieve the sufferings of our fellow man as best we can with the methods to hand...

JOHN BROWN REFILLS BRANWELL'S GLASS

BROWN: ...and third, that we do not deny each other, whatever we may be, we do not deny our brotherhood. Which is why I am here in this city.

BRANWELL: You come to...

BRANWELL DOWNS ANOTHER GLASS

BROWN: To meet with other Masons, the men of other lodges, to share a glimpse of the divine diagram, if such a phrase is not too high-fangled for a man of my station...

BRANWELL: (ENTHUSIASTIC) No, no, I believe it is not.

BROWN: We have both of us read books, Mr Branwell, from the shelves of the Mechanics' Institute.

BRANWELL: Yes! Yes!

BROWN: We Masons mean to share a glimpse of the whole, of the grand plan of the Great One. For tha must know, as we do, the proportion of Solomon's Temple in Jerusalem was no more than an imitation of the system of the natural world.

BRANWELL: (BAFFLED) Yes. I do believe so.

BROWN: Solomon's temple is the secure foundation on which all our hopes are based. The inner sanctuary alone was 20 cubits long, 20 cubits wide and 20 cubits high.

BRANWELL: (STILL BAFFLED) Why, yes!

BROWN: The holy building is a symphony. Does tha know the music of the spheres?

BRANWELL: (OVERWHELMED) I...

BROWN: (INTERRUPTING) The cube that is the base of the temple is the symbol of all the consonances in music because the ratio of its sides is one-to-one, which represents the note of unison...

BRANWELL: (NODS) Unison...

BROWN: ...or the full-string length containing within itself the vibrations of all the other musical intervals. The cube is sacred because its eight corners form the harmonic mean between its six faces and its twelve edges.

BRANWELL: (FINALLY OUTFACED) I must confess I am not so much musical as I am poetic…

BROWN: And the Holy of Holies, with its adjacent chambers, was 20 cubits broad and 30 cubits high. And the nave in front was 40 cubits long. Thus the proportions are 40 x 30 x 20. (HE DESCRIBES THE PROPORTIONS WITH HIS HANDS) These ratios are exactly the same as those which mark the musical intervals of the octave. It can therefore be said that the Temple of Solomon expressed the fundamental, the octave, the fifth and the fourth, known as the perfect consonances because they are invariable.

BRANWELL: (BAFFLED) Invariable!

BROWN: Ay, tha can believe it.

BRANWELL: I do. I do. (BEAT) Why yes. Yes. Such is a noble design. I see it all.

BROWN: Humanity itself is invariable, sir. So no man may feel himself an outcast. The true nature of humanity is invariable and homogeneous.

JOHN BROWN POURS ANOTHER GLASS FOR BRANWELL. THEN THE CHARACTERS STAGE LEFT FREEZE.

CHARLOTTE: Sisters, do not make yourselves outcasts from the world we have created.

ANNE: No, we would never do that. (BEAT) Would we, Emily?

EMILY: I wonder what he does now.

ANNE: Branwell?

EMILY: Branwell!

CHARLOTTE: Why, he prepares himself. He girds his loins
        for the battle of the morrow.

AT THE MENTION OF LOINS THE OTHER TWO
COLLAPSE IN HYSTERICAL GIGGLES

CHARLOTTE: (BRINGING THEM TO ORDER) Really, is
        this how the daughters of Gondal behave? While the
        Great Son of Angria prepares to shine in the world?
        To make his mark with study and high-mindedness?

EMILY: (IMITATING THEIR FATHER) *All their
        works they do to be seen of men.*

ANNE: (IMITATING THEIR FATHER) *Everyman's
        work shall be made manifest.*

EMILY: And he shall gird up his loins!

EMILY AND ANNE ONCE AGAIN COLLAPSE IN
GIGGLES

CHARLOTTE: (LEAPS TO HER FEET ANGRILY)
Enough!

LIGHTS GO OUT STAGE RIGHT. AT STAGE LEFT
BRANWELL SLUMPS ON THE TABLE SNORING. JOHN
BROWN GETS SLOWLY TO HIS FEET AND PUTS HIS
HAT BACK ON.

BROWN: Enough, enough. Now, now, Mr Branwell, we
        shall have to get thee to tha room. (BEAT) What was
        it our Lord Jesus said? Take no thought for the

morrow, Mr Branwell. For are we not all accounted in the Draughtsman's Great Design? Does he not see the weakness of our natures and balance them against the rest of His creation? (BEAT) Ay, let us hope He does.

JOHN BROWN TAKES HOLD OF BRANWELL, LIFTS HIM TO HIS FEET AND HALF CARRIES HIM TO EXIT STAGE LEFT. LIGHTS DIM SLOWLY UNTIL STAGE IN COMPLETE DARKNESS. TAVERN CROWD SOUND SUBSIDES. MUSIC: ALLEGRO FROM MOZART'S CONCERTO FOR BASSOON AND ORCHESTRA, OPUS 91. THEN...

ACT I, SCENE 6.

ALL LIGHTS UP. STAGE RIGHT IS THE DESK. PATRICK SITS BEHIND IT, A SCREWED-UP LETTER IN HIS HAND. STAGE LEFT IS THE TABLE WITH ALL OF THE FIGURES AND CLOTH RETURNED. ENTER BRANWELL STAGE LEFT IN TROUSERS AND WAISTCOAT. HE IS NERVOUS

BRANWELL: (SURPRISED) Father! (BEAT) I see you have...

PATRICK: (WAVES LETTER) ... taken the liberty of opening this missive. From the Leeds and Manchester Railroad Company.

BRANWELL: The Leeds...

PATRICK: (INTERRUPTING) ... and Manchester Railroad Company.

BRANWELL: My employers.

PATRICK: (WAVING LETTER) Your *former*
    employers.

BRANWELL: My *former* employers. Yes.

PATRICK: Yes, sir!

BRANWELL: Yes, father!

PATRICK: They speak of a sum of money.

BRANWELL: Yes.

PATRICK: Eleven pounds…

BRANWELL: …one shilling and sevenpence.

PATRICK: …one shilling and seven pence. You are
correct, sir. How I wish you had been correct very much
earlier!

BRANWELL: I would have told you…

PATRICK: Would you, sir? (BEAT) Yes, I am sure you
    would. After a fashion. After the fashion of your
    telling me about your interview at the Royal
    Academy…

BRANWELL: (HE TURNS TO THE TABLE,
    NERVOUSLY PICKS UP A SOLDIER) I believe
    there was a prejudice against me, sir. I fear that, being
    Londoners, they look down on northerners at the
    Royal Academy. The sons of…

PATRICK: Parsons? Well, yes, perhaps they do.

BRANWELL: I meant sons of *northerners*, sir. I did not seek
    to blame you, nor other parsons, beyond the general…

PATRICK: (INTERRUPTING) But perhaps it is true in
            some areas. Perhaps the Bradford patrons of your
            artist's workshop did not warm to the paintings of a
            parson's son. They, after all, have little reason to rail
            at northerners. No, sir. Their geography, I think,
            would argue against it.

BRANWELL: (PICKS UP SECOND SOLDIER WITH
            OTHER HAND, HOLDS THE TWO OF THEM
            CLOSELY, FACE TO FACE) I cannot deny my
            failure in the business of portraiture. Though many of
            my artistic friends – Mr Leyland the sculptor and his
            brother Francis for example – have often described
            my work in the most generous terms, frequently
            invoking the name of Mr Gainsborough.

GRINNING, HE MANIPULATES THE SOLDIERS SO
THEY APPEAR TO BE SPARRING, THEN HIS FACE
BECOMES DOWNCAST AND HE THROWS THEM
BACK ON THE TABLE

BRANWELL: The world of art is difficult, sir, at the best of
            times. There are fashions, modes, styles that must be
            caught at the instant, to make one appear attractive to
            the hoi polloi. If one is inclined to finer things, the
            matter of a Renaissance sensibility, certain eternal
            truths, then…

PATRICK: Eternal truths, sir? What about catching the
            likeness of a sitter? Surely that is the main truth
            required in portraiture? Or am I become old-fangled,
            sir? (PAUSE) Well, what exactly would you
            categorise as eternal truths?

BRANWELL: Surely, sir, the brotherhood of mankind in which we honour and accept each other in every degree and kind and appetite...

PATRICK: That sounds to me, sir, like chapel talk, the rants of the radicals, the erstwhile revolutionaries of France...

BRANWELL: Was not Wordsworth himself a supporter of that revolution? (QUOTES) Oh what a joy to be alive but to be young was very heaven!

PATRICK: Heaven, sir, does not reside across the English Channel!

BRANWELL: (SUBDUED) No, sir.

PATRICK: No, sir. (HE ALSO BECOMES SUBDUED) But I do accept your point that many of our greatest artists have suffered to be ignored much of their lives. (BEAT) It may still turn out, sir, that you are one of these. (PAUSE) But you are not, it seems, one of our greatest *accountants*! (HE WAVES THE LETTER AGAIN)

BRANWELL: No, sir.

PATRICK: How could you have permitted this to happen, this loss of revenue revealed by the auditors? Surely the post of ticket clerk is not so arduous...

BRANWELL: No indeed.

PATRICK: Nor so irksome...

BRANWELL: The clerking of tickets on the railway is an honourable post, father, and has many satisfactions. I was often praised during my employment for the elegance of my handwriting and the neatness of my style...

PATRICK: Pish! Your artistic friends again! (BEAT) You could *write* a ledger, it seems, at least enough so you caught the likeness. But could not *read* one adequately.

BRANWELL: No, sir. (HE BEGINS TO DRAW CIRCLES WITH HIS FINGERS ON THE TABLECLOTH) It was during that period when I was most prodigious in my poetic output, father, and perhaps my attention wandered from mundane matters. (BEAT) I remember now. I was translating Horace from the Latin.

PATRICK: Perhaps Horace is therefore to blame. But it is *we* will rue the day.

BRANWELL: (HE FACES THE AUDIENCE AND STANDS IN DECLAIMING MODE, HIS ARMS OUTSTRETCHED) To Sestius. (PAUSE) Rough winter melts beneath the breeze of spring/ Refitted ships shun not the silent sea/ Nor man nor beasts to folds or firesides cling/ Nor hoar frosts whiten over field and tree.

PATRICK GETS UP SLOWLY, WALKS ACROSS TO BRANWELL AND EMBRACES HIM

PATRICK: (HIS MOOD WHOLLY CHANGED) My brilliant son!

BRANWELL: Thankyou, father. I thought it caught the original...

PATRICK: …likeness. Yes, I believe it did.

BRANWELL: ... yet newly fashioned in a selection of language properly used by modern man. As Mr Wordsworth says all modern poetry should be! (BEAT) I will find a new post, father. (BEAT) I have made a good friend among the railway folk. There is one called Jacob who will…

PATRICK: (ANGRY AGAIN) Railway folk! Enough! No more clerking, sir, no more railways! (BEAT) A teaching post. That is what we must seek. It may well be you can inspire others. As I believe your sisters will. They are all bent on being governesses. (BEAT) Yes, yes. It is the only way forward.

LIGHTS DIM. SPOTLIGHTS COME UP ON PATRICK AND BRANWELL

BRANWELL: Yes. Teaching. You are right, father. It is an honourable profession and has many satisfactions.

PATRICK: It is agreed then.

BRANWELL: It is agreed. Yes. It is agreed, father.

THEY EMBRACE. SPOTLIGHTS FADE SO STAGE IS IN DARKNESS AGAIN. MUSIC.

CHOIR SINGS: He who would valiant be/Gainst all disaster/ Let him in constancy/ Follow the master./There's no discouragement/ shall make him once relent/ His first avowed intent/ To be a pilgrim.

ACT I, SCENE 7.

SINGING FADES, THEN THERE IS BIRDSONG.
SPOTLIGHT COMES UP ON JOHN BROWN, WEARING
LABOURER'S CLOTHES, SITTING DOWNSTAGE
CENTRE, SMOKING A CLAY PIPE. HIS SHOVEL IS
LYING CLOSE BY. SECOND SPOT FOLLOWS
PATRICK, IN OVERCOAT, AS HE ENTERS STAGE
RIGHT. HE CARRIES A WALKING STICK AND WALKS
SLOWLY TO WHERE BROWN IS SITTING.

PATRICK: Brown.

BROWN: (WITHOUT LOOKING UP) Parson.

PATRICK: Are there no more graves to be dug?

BROWN: Even a man of *my* calling must take his rest,
         parson. (LAUGHS)

PATRICK: I believe you are often here at this time of
day.

BROWN: (LOOKS UP AT PATRICK) When fate
         allows. (LOOKS SKYWARD) When the Great
         Geometer permits me.

PATRICK: And I believe on occasion you encounter my
         son.

BROWN: Young Mr Branwell enjoys his daily
         ambulation, it is true. Ay, on occasion…

PATRICK: You meet. And present him with a package.

BROWN: At his *request*. Always at *his* request.

PATRICK: No more!

BROWN: (SNIGGERS) No more? Can any man say that to a gravedigger? Not even a parson.

PATRICK: (ANGRY) You forget yourself!

BROWN: (STANDING UP) Sir, I mean no offence. Young Mr Branwell considers me his friend. (BEAT) Sir, why do you pursue him so? Is it not enough that he is part of this world, this great symmetry? Why not permit him his small radius, his tangent, his complementary angle?

PATRICK: *I* do not consider you his friend.

BROWN: I am sorry for that, sir. For I consider myself a friend to everyone, all the inhabitants of this great sphere, this world of ours.

PATRICK: This world of *yours*. Not mine, nor my son's. (BEAT) I know you, Brown.

BROWN: And I know you, sir. And I know your son.

PATRICK: My son who can scarce dress himself by the middle of the day.

BROWN: (STANDING UP NOW) *I* will dress him, sir. I will be his manservant.

PATRICK RAISES HIS STICK FOR A MOMENT, THEN THINKS BETTER OF IT. HE WALKS SLOWLY STAGE LEFT, FOLLOWED BY SPOT, THEN HALTS AND TURNS

PATRICK: I know you, sir! I know you! Do not doubt that I do!

EXIT PATRICK SLOWLY STAGE LEFT

BROWN: (CUPS HIS HAND TO HIS EAR) What?
(LAUGHS) I do not hear thee. I hear nowt. Speak up
now, Parson! What, sir? What? I do not hear thee!

JOHN BROWN GRINS, PUFFS AT HIS PIPE, PICKS UP
HIS SHOVEL AND FOLLOWS PATRICK SLOWLY
STAGE LEFT, EXITS. SPOTS DIM TO COMPLETE
DARKNESS AND SILENCE.

END OF ACT I

ACT II, SCENE 1.

LIGHTS COME UP ON STUDY AS IN ACT I.
BRANWELL IN DRESSING GOWN SLUMPED AT DESK
STAGE RIGHT. SOLDIERS AND OTHER FIGURES LAID
OUT ON TABLE STAGE LEFT. BRANWELL STIRS.

BRANWELL: (LOOKS ROUND, CONFUSED) What?
What, sir? What? I do not hear you! I do not hear you!
(HE RUBS HIS EYES) A dream! (FOCUSES) But is
not all of it a dream then? (BEAT) No, no, it is not.
(BEAT) I must write! My novel! Where is my novel?
I must work. (SEARCHES THE DRAWERS, FINDS
SHEAF OF PAPER) Here! Ah, yes! Yes! (HE
SPREADS OUT THE PAGES AND BEGINS TO
READ) Book One, Chapter 17. In the House.
(CLEARS HIS THROAT AND READS) He made no
halt in his intrusion on the quietude of the Hall. He
was received by the Lady of the Mansion in the
breakfast room... (BEAT) *Breakfast* room? The
library, perhaps, is more elegant. No, no. Breakfast is
more *intimate*. (READS) No servant could have been
so dull as not to perceive the change in their calm and
sweet-tempered mistress. The dove-like eye now
seemed troubled; the voice with its gentle tone, now
gave way to hesitation... (BEAT) *Gave way* to
hesitation? *Harboured* hesitation? No. No. *Gave way*.
(BEAT) This is good. It stands the test of time.
(READS) She recalled the promise lately given to her
furious husband, but a still small voice told the lady
that her visitor had feelings of a wider, higher and
deeper range than her... (HE WAVES A HAND IN
FRONT OF HIS FACE) Her *husband*? Her *spouse*?
Spouse, then! Still, small, voice. Yes, spouse is more
alliterative with those adjacent words. (BEAT) Lady?
Wife? No, no! Lady! Told the *lady*. There. Keep it.

The *l* and the *d* are most evocative. There! (HE
WRITES)

BRANWELL SITS BACK IN HIS CHAIR, REACHES OUT
FOR THE DECANTER, THINKS BETTER OF IT

BRANWELL: Now, something of a contrast. (BEAT)
Where? (SHUFFLES THE MANUSCRIPT) Book
Two, Chapter Three. In the Garden. (READS) It was
late August and the sun was still warm. He turned the
corner by the daffodils and came once more upon the
lady. (BEAT) Daffodils? Chrysanthemums? Perhaps
chrysanthemums are more in accord with the seasons.
But I am not so much a naturalist as I am a novelist.
And the daffodils might be well nigh spent. Yes, yes,
it is therefore a more telling image. (WRITES, THEN
READS) She turned, affrighted, at the sound of his
footfall and leaned against the tall ash tree. (BEAT)
Ash? Oak? Oak is masculine but perhaps too much
for one so genteel. Ash then. Leave it.

HE PUTS DOWN THE NOVEL, AGAIN REACHES OUT
FOR THE DECANTER, AGAIN THINKS BETTER OF IT

BRANWELL: Well, there it is, Mr Editor. Soon it shall
wend its way towards your publishing house. If only
life were as elegant and as wholesome as my novel,
Mr Editor, as the novels which fall – plop! – on your
desk every day. But in life… In *my* life… (HE PICKS
UP ANOTHER SHEET OF PAPER AND READS)
Leyland, my old friend, sculptor and scholar, teacher
of my art… (BEAT) I have to tell you there is a lady
about whom I have high hopes though much
concealed. She has been until recently, I confess to
you, a married woman, but this state is no more. Her
husband, my erstwhile employer, has lately shaken off

this mortal coil, as Mr Shakespeare says. I therefore wait each day, breathless, to hear from her. I wait... (BEAT) But she is surrounded by powerful persons who hate me. The husband has left his property in trust to the widow provided I do not see her. If I disobey, it is to ruin her. But I dare hope she will take courage. I can make my own way in the world and have written again to the railway company to reconsider their decision to release me... (HE GAZES INTO MIDDLE DISTANCE) Though I write about a love concealed, I tell you truly no servant could have been so dull as not to perceive the change in their calm and sweet-tempered mistress. The dove-like eye seemed troubled; the voice with its gentle tone gave way to hesitation... (BEAT) To tear from my heart the thousand recollections of her that rush upon me would be to steal from a newly blind man his remembrance of sunlight. (BEAT) Yes. Yes. That's good.

BRANWELL DROPS THE PAPER ON THE DESK, GETS UP, WALKS ACROSS TO THE TABLE, STARES DOWN AT THE TOY SOLDIERS. HE PICKS UP TWO OF THEM.

BRANWELL: Leyland, old friend, it would be disheartening to work myself up again to new battles. I have already been compelled to retreat with heavy loss and no gain. My army stands now where it did then, and I mourn the slaughter of my youth and hope.

HE WALKS SLOWLY BACK TO THE DESK, DROPS THE SOLDIERS ON THE DESK, SITS DOWN, TAKES UP THE PAPER ONCE MORE. LIGHTS DIM STAGE LEFT.

BRANWELL: While I am thus writing, old friend and tutor, may I also mention my embarrassment with an outstanding bill at The Old Cock in Halifax. It is a mere three shillings, but I have been threatened with a court summons. You yourself are a valued customer. I wonder if you might reassure the landlady of my reliability in such matters? (SIGNS IT) Your good and faithful friend as ever, P.B. Bronte.

BRANWELL DROPS THE LETTER ON THE DESK, PICKS UP ANOTHER SHEET OF PAPER, STUDIES IT FOR A MOMENT

BRANWELL   (READS) Oh, Lydia, my love, mistress of my heart... I have to tell you that you are a lady about whom I have high hopes though much concealed. (BEAT) You have been until recently a married woman, but this state is no more. I do hope your husband, now he is freed from the dungeon of this life, as was Christian in Mr Bunyan's tale, will receive in heaven that honour and respect for every degree, kind and appetite which is sadly absent here on earth. (BEAT) Meanwhile I wait each day, breathless, to hear from you. You are surrounded by powerful persons who hate me. Yet I dare hope you will take courage and reveal your true self to me. (BEAT) Though our love has long been a love concealed on both our parts, yet no servant could have been so dull as not to perceive the change in your calm and sweet-tempered demeanour... (BEAT) To tear from my heart the thousand recollections of you would be to steal from a newly blind man his remembrance of sunlight. (BEAT) Also, I have written a poem, which I enclose. (BEAT) Where is it?

HE SCRABBLES IN ONE OF THE DRAWERS, PULLS OUT A FEW SHEETS OF PAPER

BRANWELL: (HE STANDS, CLEARS HIS THROAT
        AND READS) I see your picture is cleverly made/
        Where should be sunshine, there is shade/ And from
        your heart your smiles still shine/ though you have
        stolen all from mine.

BRANWELL PRESSES A HAND TO HIS HEART AND
SMILES WITH SATISFACTION. THEN HE RESUMES
READING THE LETTER

BRANWELL: And I have sent a copy already to the
        Bradford Herald! I await their letter of acceptance.
        (WRITES) Your stout-hearted servant, PB Bronte.

BRANWELL DROPS THE LETTER ON THE DESK, SITS
DOWN, REACHES FOR THE DECANTER, FILLS THE
GLASS AND EMPTIES IT. THERE IS A SUDDEN SOUND
OF A WOMAN'S LOUD SOBBING.

ACT II, SCENE 2.

LIGHTS GO UP STAGE LEFT REVEALING CHARLOTTE
STANDING BEHIND THE TABLE, WEEPING, A LETTER
IN HER HAND

BRANWELL: (SHOCKED) Charlotte! Sister! (ALARMED)
        What is it? (HE GETS UP, RUSHES OVER AND
        EMBRACES HER) Oh my poor Mary Percy! Let
        Zamorna comfort you!

CHARLOTTE: (SHE PULLS AWAY FROM HIM) I do not
        need the comfort of Zamorna! I do not need the
        comfort of a toy soldier!

BRANWELL: (HE ALSO PULLS AWAY) Sister, do not reject me! Do not leave me in my misery.

CHARLOTTE: (ANGRY) *Your* misery! (GAZES TO HEAVEN) *Branwell's* misery! What misery is that? The misery of the table-top? The blood and tears of toyland? Or were those real battles we fought here? Was this wood once truly stained with the lifeblood of the infantry? Because I look, I look, and I cannot see the stains. (BEAT) Nor do I smell the smoke of cannon. I sniff the fuggy air and smell only the sourness of gin!

BRANWELL: I have had a *glass*, sister! That is all. (BEAT) To help with my writing.

CHARLOTTE: I have not read your writing for many a year, brother. For now it is sealed away in an envelope and bears a new-fangled postage stamp. You write *letters*, Branwell! Not that you ever post them.

BRANWELL: (FEEBLY) No, no, I do not write only *letters*. You mistake me. I am a *man* of letters. (LAUGHS) I would not want you to think I write only letters. No. No. (BEAT) Poems. I write poems. At this very moment, I wait on acceptance from the local paper.

CHARLOTTE: Poems! (BEAT) And what is your subject?

BRANWELL: My subject is love!

CHARLOTTE: A noble subject. (LAUGHS) *Girls'* games! Are not the games of love mere girls' games?

BRANWELL: These are no games! I do not *play* at love!

CHARLOTTE: Do you not? (BEAT) Does someone then play with *you*?

BRANWELL: I do not understand.

CHARLOTTE: I also do not understand. (BEAT) There is always love. Else what will the soldiers do when they have won? They must have something to do when the battle is over. (BEAT) You write your letters, brother, and I write mine! (SHE HOLDS UP THE CRUMPLED LETTER) But I *post* mine!

BRANWELL: (CONFUSED) *Your* letter?

CHARLOTTE: My own! Sent back to me. (BEAT) A rejection from the publisher of my heart.

BRANWELL: (HE RETREATS TO THE DESK AND SITS DOWN) I said I do not understand.

CHARLOTTE: I will show you then. I will explain. It will not make pretty reading. It is not at all like Miss Austen.

CHARLOTTE FOLLOWS HIM TO THE DESK, DRAGGING ACROSS A CHAIR, SITS DOWN AND PLACES THE LETTER ON THE DESK IN FRONT OF HIM

CHARLOTTE: Look. (POINTS TO LETTER) It is a long time since you have read what *I* write, brother. These are the kind of letters *I* write!

BRANWELL: (TURNING AWAY) If these are words of moment, sister, if these are words close to your heart and person, then I would feel an intruder to read them.

CHARLOTTE: If you will not read them, *I* will read them to you. (BEAT) Your subject is love. And so is mine.

BRANWELL: And to whom do you write of your love?

CHARLOTTE: My professor.

BRANWELL: I do not...

CHARLOTTE: ...understand? You keep saying so, brother, yet I think you *do* understand. Else I would not bother with you. Now. Listen (SHE BEGINS TO READ) I have done everything. I have sought occupation. I have denied myself absolutely the pleasure of speaking about you. But I have been able to conquer neither my regrets nor my impatience. (SHE TURNS TO BRANWELL) Is this familiar to you, brother? Does this strike a chord with your emotions? With your poetic intellect?

BRANWELL: Your professor? You mean...

CHARLOTTE: Monsieur Constantine. The constant one. The head of my school. Where I worked and taught. (BEAT) And *learned*.

BRANWELL: The monsieur. The Belgian! (HE IS HORRIFIED) You have formed an attachment with a Belgian?

CHARLOTTE: The *monsieur*. Yes. We all called him that.

BRANWELL: But he is (BEAT) foreign. And (BEAT) a member of the Church of Rome!

CHARLOTTE: I have heard that *Byron* died a Catholic. Though you would not notice from his verses.

BRANWELL: (EMBARRASSED) Sister, do not continue. It is unseemly that you divulge this...

CHARLOTTE: ...passion?

BRANWELL: ...liaison.

CHARLOTTE: Oh. And I thought you did not know your French. Strange how the English always find a French word to describe the very thing of which they disapprove. (BEAT) But your new poem... Is *that* in English?

BRANWELL: Of course it is in English.

CHARLOTTE: And the whole world may read it? Whichever part of the world buys the Halifax Guardian?

BRANWELL: It is the Bradford Herald!

CHARLOTTE: Touché! (BEAT) There. Another French word for your vocabulary. (BEAT) My own French is tres pauvre, I'm afraid. When I write in French, the monsieur corrects my sentences. (LAUGHS BITTERLY) Sometimes also when I write in *English*.

BRANWELL: Believe me – your English sentences are excellent.

CHARLOTTE: (ICILY) Thank you.

BRANWELL: But in my case we speak of a poem. We speak of rhyme and metre...

CHARLOTTE: Assonance and alliteration, no doubt.

BRANWELL: Perhaps. Though at this moment I forget some details of the style...

CHARLOTTE: But not the content! You do not forget the content!

BRANWELL: (PUTTING HIS HEAD IN HIS HANDS) I do not forget the content.

CHARLOTTE: The hurt! (BEAT) We none of us forget the hurt!

BRANWELL: This thing of yours is not a poem. This is...

CHARLOTTE: A letter. Naked. For a letter does not wear the garments of rhyme and metre.

BRANWELL: And you are not a poet! You are a woman! And women...

CHARLOTTE: ... must not talk of such things. Women must not show themselves naked. Not even in words. (BEAT) But you have *seen* me naked, brother. Is that not so?

BRANWELL When we were *children*. We are not children now.

CHARLOTTE: Are we not? I can never make up my mind about that. (BEAT) But yes, you are right. A letter is always naked if it is sincere. It can never pretend to be a poem. (BEAT) But listen how it speaks to you. (SHE READS) It is indeed humiliating to be unable to control one's thoughts, to be the slave of regret, of memory, the slave of a fixed and dominant idea which lords it over the mind. (BEAT) Your last letter was a stay and prop to me, nourishment for half a year...

BRANWELL: (AGITATED) Stop. This is unseemly.

CHARLOTTE: (HER VOICE RISING) To forbid me to write to you, to refuse to answer me, would be to tear from me my only joy on earth, to deprive me of my final privilege. Believe me, my master, so long as I believe you are pleased with me, so long as I have hope of receiving news from you, I can be at rest and not too sad. But when day by day I await a letter and when day by day disappointment flings me back in overwhelming sorrow, then fever claims me...

BRANWELL: Stop!

CHARLOTTE: (HER VOICE REACHING A CRESCENDO) ...I lose appetite and sleep. I pine away.

BRANWELL: (DESPERATE NOW) Stop!

CHARLOTTE STOPS READING, SHE HOLDS THE LETTER UP IN THE AIR.

CHARLOTTE: He sent it back. As you see. It was unopened.

SHE CRUMPLES IT AND THROWS IT TO THE FLOOR

BRANWELL: Perhaps his wife...

CHARLOTTE: Of *course* his wife! (BEAT) But is he not a man? Does he not have the courage...?

BRANWELL: It is *well* that he sends it back. He has done right by you. I am your brother. And a poet. And I can see that words which may flow in perfect innocence from a young lady like yourself might with others be taken amiss.

CHARLOTTE: How?

BRANWELL: They might be thought to mean more than they do. They might be thought to take on a (BEAT) *carnal* aspect.

CHARLOTTE: A carnal aspect? Is this how modern poets write of love? (BEAT) And if that carnal aspect were true?

BRANWELL: Charlotte, you besmirch yourself to talk like this!

CHARLOTTE: Because I am not a man? Because a woman must never confess to a carnal aspect? (SHE LAUGHS)

BRANWELL: You are not yourself. That is the fact of the matter. You have been upset...

CHARLOTTE: *Deeply* upset.

BRANWELL: *Deeply* upset (BEAT) by this letter. But sanity will return.

CHARLOTTE: To which of us, brother? To which of us will sanity return? (BEAT) I think sometimes pain has its own intelligence, that it seeks out those who are weak in this or that way and devises a narrow strategy for each of us. (BEAT) To be rejected! That was always the worst fear for me. And my pain, my very clever pain, knows this. But I have cast it down, this pain, this sorrow, I have crumpled it and cast it on the floor and I will walk across the room and step on it.

SHE WALKS SLOWLY OVER TO WHERE SHE THREW THE LETTER AND STUBS IT WITH HER TOE, LIKE STUBBING OUT A CIGARETTE

CHARLOTTE: (MALEVOLENTLY) Of *course* it's his wife!

BRANWELL: (SUDDENLY) My Lydia is not like that.

CHARLOTTE: (SURPRISED) What?

BRANWELL: My Lydia knows my pain and comforts me.
(BEAT) But there are others. There are those who
hate me. They surround her. They whisper about me.
Now her husband is dead. And I am sorry for it. For I
wish no man harm. Yet I see the hand of God in it all.

CHARLOTTE: (AMAZED) *The hand of God?* (SHE
LAUGHS) Lydia? (IT DAWNS) Your *employer's
wife!* (BEAT) How alike we are, you and I. We go out
into the world and we take our madness with us.

BRANWELL: It is *not* madness!

CHARLOTTE: What a vile, corrupt breed we teachers are!
All of us who think we have something to give the
world. We give only our insanity. (BEAT) How often
does she write?

BRANWELL: I tell you. There are those close to her who
hate me. It is difficult for her to write.

CHARLOTTE: (WITH A RESIGNED SMILE) Difficult!
What is there in life that is not difficult?

CHARLOTTE WALKS ACROSS TO BRANWELL AND
CRADLES HIS HEAD ON HER BREAST

CHARLOTTE: We are still friends, it seems. Good. I thought
for a while we were not.

BRANWELL HUGS HER, LIKE A TODDLER HUGGING
ITS MOTHER

BRANWELL: We will *always* be friends. We are alike.

CHARLOTTE: Even though you are a boy and boys have
        larger brains?

BRANWELL: (LAUGHS) Even so.

CHARLOTTE: Well, I suppose you are right. We have no
        secrets. We have seen each other naked. When we
        were children. (BEAT) And are we not still children
        now?

THEY EMBRACE GENTLY. LIGHTS GO DOWN. MUSIC:
CHOPIN: BALLADE I, OPUS 23.

ACT II, SCENE 3.

MUSIC FADES. LIGHTS GO UP. THE NEXT SECTION
COMPRISES TWO SEPARATE SCENES VIEWED
SIMULTANEOUSLY, AND THE CHARACTERS IN
EACH TAKE TURNS TO SPEAK. THE BRONTE GIRLS
AND PATRICK ARE GATHERED ROUND THE DESK
STAGE RIGHT. EMILY AND ANNE WEAR BRIGHTER
DRESSES THAN PREVIOUSLY, THOUGH EMILY STILL
WEARS A HEAD SCARF AND THE BROOM IS
LEANING AGAINST THE DESK. PATRICK SITS ON A
CHAIR, FROM THE BACK OF WHICH HANGS
BRANWELL'S DRESSING GOWN, WHILE EMILY SITS
ON THE DESK SWINGING HER LEGS. ANNE AND
CHARLOTTE STAND. THE GIRLS HOLD TUMBLERS
AND THERE IS A JUG OF FRUIT JUICE ON THE DESK.

PATRICK HOLDS A WINE GLASS AND THERE IS A
DECANTER OF WINE ALSO ON THE DESK.

THE TABLE STAGE LEFT OF THE LAST SCENE HAS
HAD THE FIGURES REMOVED AND ON IT THERE IS A
MEDIEVAL SWORD AND A LARGE BOOK
DECORATED WITH OCCULT SIGNS. ALSO A PEWTER
JUG AND TWO SPIRIT GLASSES

PATRICK: It is good to have my family about me.
          Christmas is a time for families.

CHARLOTTE: I am sure Branwell will be back shortly,
father.

EMILY: There is, I believe, some revelry in the
          village. The Christmas Eve sort that involves the men.

ANNE: You mean involves strong drink.

CHARLOTTE: But I am sure he will be back tonight.

EMILY: Or early tomorrow. In time for his presents,
          no doubt. I am giving him my old copy of A
          Christmas Carol. To remind him what Christmas is
          about.

ANNE: I know the one you mean. The spine is torn
          and you have pencilled many comments in the
          margins. That is not much of a Christmas present,
          Emily. He will think you are a veritable Jacob Marley.

EMILY: Let him think rather I am the Spirit of
          Christmas Yet to Come. That might do him some
          good.

PATRICK: Oh come now. Branwell is a young man. And young men...

EMILY: (INTERRUPTING) No, no. He is *not* so young. He merely affects to be young. He still keeps toy soldiers in his drawer.

PATRICK: You are harsh with him at times.

EMILY: No more than he deserves. No more than *you*, father.

PATRICK: I am tired. I will drain this glass and retire to bed. (HE DRINKS) I am grown old. Once I could control his ways. Once I could control *your* ways, daughters. Now I must let you come and go as you please. But Branwell is still my son.

THE CHARACTERS STAGE RIGHT FREEZE

THREE LOUD KNOCKS. ENTER UPSTAGE LEFT BRANWELL, DRESSED IN A WHITE ROBE AND BLINDFOLD, LED BY JOHN BROWN IN A BLACK BARRISTER'S GOWN. THEY COME TO A STOP EITHER SIDE OF THE TABLE, JOHN BROWN ON THE FAR STAGE LEFT SIDE

BROWN: Welcome, my son. Welcome, my brother. Welcome.

BRANWELL: (HE PUTS HIS HANDS TOGETHER IN SIGN OF PRAYER) Thanks to you, father. Thanks to you, brother.

BROWN: Today is the day, my son, my brother, to receive from thy holy father and true brother the rites of initiation. Does tha wish that? Does tha wish to join us in the true knowledge?

BRANWELL: With all my heart.

BROWN: Tha's been divested already of what monies tha carried, so tha comes to this temple bereft of the help and support of this world.

BRANWELL: I have. I do.

BROWN: Then let the ritual begin. (PAUSE) Thee is a poor candidate in a state of darkness...

BRANWELL: I am.

BROWN: And tha comes of tha own free will and accord, humbly soliciting to be admitted to the mysteries and privileges of Freemasonry...

BRANWELL: I do.

BROWN: Kneel.

BRANWELL: I will.

HE DOES SO. JOHN BROWN PICKS UP THE SWORD AND TOUCHES BOTH BRANWELL'S SHOULDERS IN TURN, LIKE A MONARCH BESTOWING KNIGHTHOOD. THEN HE PUTS THE SWORD BACK ON THE TABLE, PICKS UP THE BOOK AND READS FROM IT

BROWN: Tha must know that all men are a measure of the world...

BRANWELL: I know.

BROWN: It is their only value and significance.

BRANWELL: So I have learned.

BROWN: They reflect the perfect proportions of the Great Geometer...

THEY FREEZE

ANNE: I wish he would see the error of his ways. But he has no sense of proportion.

PATRICK: Come, daughter. It is the season of good will.

CHARLOTTE: (SHARPLY) And we do not wish to worry our father unduly.

PATRICK: You are all of you young women of great virtue. Sometimes it is hard for a young woman to understand the nature of a man. But I... (BEAT) though I am old and somewhat damaged by the world, I do understand Branwell, I *do*.

CHARLOTTE: It is a phase. It will pass. It is like a wild passage in a concerto by Vivaldi. It will be replaced by a slower movement. That is the nature of music. The fast and the slow. It will calm him.

EMILY: But Branwell only listens to the music in his head.

CHARLOTTE: He is not the only one in this family who does so. Not the only one who *dances* to it.

EMILY: If you mean *me*, sister...

CHARLOTTE: I do.

EMILY: Dancer, indeed! I did not think to cut such a
           dashing figure!

THEY FREEZE

BROWN: All men are mere figures and fractions. Is not
           an inch the length of thy fingernail?

BRANWELL: It is.

BROWN: And twelve the length of thy foot?

BRANWELL: Yes, yes.

BROWN: And a yard is the measure of thine arm and
           thy leg and thy reach and thy stride?

BRANWELL: Yes.

BROWN: Is not a stone that weighs a pound the natural
           limit of thy grasp and lift? Why does tha seek to lift
           more?

BRANWELL: I do not.

BROWN: But once tha did. Once tha sought to move
           mountains.

BRANWELL: No longer.

BROWN: Tha's become a sounding brass and a tinkling
           cymbal.

BRANWELL: I renounce those ways.

BROWN: And what is now thine ambition?

BRANWELL: To be as all my brothers, my fellow men. To be no more then the lowest.

BROWN: I rejoice to hear it.

BRANWELL: I also rejoice.

THEY FREEZE

PATRICK: We should rejoice! We should not have such long faces. We should rejoice in our saviour who has put us on this earth to do good works.

ANNE: (SUDDENLY ALERT) Good works! Why, yes, our good works should be celebrated. Father...

CHARLOTTE: (INTERRUPTING) But it is never right that we should *boast* of our good works, sister. Such an action brings demerit upon them and upon ourselves. (TO EMILY) Does it not, sister?

EMILY: Charlotte is right. Whited sepulchres are never pleasing to the Lord.

ANNE: But sometimes, when the news is good, is it not our duty to communicate it? Would it not raise people's spirits if it were known?

CHARLOTTE: And others might be condemned to purgatory. Better sometimes to keep secrets, sister. At least till time is ripe.

PATRICK: Secrets? You bemuse me with your talk. What secrets can young women of virtue ever have? You jest with an old man. (HE LAUGHS)

THEY FREEZE

BROWN: This is the secret which we now share with
        thee. For we are entering a new age when all
        numbers shall be levelled and all shall be as one! (HE
        PUTS DOWN THE BOOK AND REMOVES
        BRANWELL'S BLINDFOLD) Look around thee,
        lad. Gaze upon thy new world.

BRANWELL: (GAZING ONLY AT JOHN BROWN) The
        world. It is beautiful.

BROWN: But do not seek to be more than tha can be.
        Be humble. Any help and support tha may receive can
        only come now as a gift from thy fellow Masons.
        (BEAT) Here, let us now take God's gift of wine by
        which thy new life may be consecrated.

JOHN BROWN TAKES THE JUG AND GLASSES AND
POURS THE WINE. WE HEAR THE OVERTURE FROM
MOZART'S MAGIC FLUTE

LIGHTS DIM. THE WHOLE STAGE BECOMES DARK.
THERE IS SILENCE

ACT II, SCENE 4.

LIGHTS GO UP ON SAME SCENE. STAGE RIGHT:
EMILY IS STANDING BY THE DESK, HOLDING A
LARGE PAPERBACK BOOK COVERED IN BROWN
PAPER AND BEARING THE LEGEND *PRINTER'S
PROOF*. CHARLOTTE IS SEATED ON THE CHAIR
VACATED BY PATRICK. STAGE LEFT: ANNE IS
SITTING OVER BY THE TABLE TO WHICH THE
SOLDIERS AND CLOTH HAVE BEEN RETURNED

EMILY: (READING FROM THE BOOK) This is
        certainly a beautiful country! In all England I do not

believe I could have fixed on a situation so completely removed from the stir of society.

ANNE: (TO EMILY) Well done, Mr Bell! Well done, Wuthering Heights! I see from the very start of your novel that you draw strongly upon your own life and situation, sir.

CHARLOTTE: (TO EMILY) You could not be further removed, sir, from the stir of society than to be here with your sisters...

ANNE: Brothers!

CHARLOTTE: Brothers! Brother writers! The Bells! (POINTS TO EMILY) Ellis Bell! (POINTS TO ANNE) Acton Bell! (POINTS TO HERSELF) Currer Bell!

ANNE: The Bells of the ball!

THE GIRLS LAUGH

CHARLOTTE: (TO EMILY) Come, be not so shy. Let us have more.

EMILY: Which passage do you request?

CHARLOTTE: Why, it should be something involving that eccentric Mr Heathcliff! Do you not think so, Anne? For he has fast become my favourite character in all English fiction.

ANNE: Your favourite *male* character, you mean!

EMILY: Let me see. (TURNS THE PAGES) Well, I shall risk this one, if it please you. Though it is hardly festive reading. (SHE READS) "I shall join you directly," said Heathcliff, "Keep out of the yard, though. The dogs are unchained." I obeyed, as far as to quit the chamber; when I was witness, involuntarily, to a piece of superstition which belied oddly Mr Heathcliff's apparent sense. He got onto the bed and wrenched open the lattice, bursting as he pulled at it into an uncontrollable passion of tears. "Come in, come in!" he sobbed, "Cathy, do come! Oh do – once more! Oh my heart's darling! Hear me this time!" The spectre gave no sign of being, but the snow and wind whirled wildly through, blowing out the light.

ANNE: Ghosts are ever a part of Christmas, are they not? Oh, it makes me shiver!

CHARLOTTE: It makes us *all* shiver! (TO EMILY) But do I not see in the character of your Mr Heathcliff a reflection of your own demeanour, Mr Bell?

ANNE: (TO EMILY) He is always brooding, like yourself, Mr Bell. He has that air of Lord Byron...

CHARLOTTE: (TO EMILY) Is it not a self-portrait, Mr Bell? Will it not perhaps become a bad influence on the younger generation of women? Will it not set the minds of young girls a-racing?

ANNE: (TO EMILY) Their hearts a-fluttering!

CHARLOTTE: (TO EMILY) Their hair streaming back in the wind as they run across the heather-strewn moors?

ANNE: (TO EMILY) Dreaming of their own Mr Heathcliff?

THEY COLLAPSE IN LAUGHTER AGAIN

CHARLOTTE: (TO EMILY) Well, sir, and what do you say to us?

EMILY: I do not write for young girls, sir. If they should succumb to such bestial charms...

ANNE: Bestial charms! Why, that is a phrase to be savoured, Mr Bell.

CHARLOTTE: (TO EMILY) Then for whom *do* you write?

EMILY: (THINKS A MOMENT) I write for myself, Mr Bell.

CHARLOTTE: (TO EMILY) How selfish of you, Mr Bell! (BEAT) But sometimes perhaps we *must* be selfish. We must do things for ourselves.

EMILY: We?

ANNE: Women. Do you mean women, Mr Bell?

CHARLOTTE: What do *I* know of women, Mr Bell? I who am a *bachelor*? (BEAT) Come, let us hear from your own celebrated work. Let us hear from Agnes Grey.

EMILY CROSSES THE STAGE TO SIT IN ANNE'S PLACE. ANNE REPLACES HER BY THE DESK. ANNE ALSO HAS A LARGE PAPERBACK BOUND IN BROWN PAPER WITH *PRINTER'S PROOF* PRINTED ON IT

EMILY: (TO ANNE) Read me the part where she decides to leave home. I like that.

ANNE: (THUMBS THROUGH THE BOOK, STARTS READING) "I should like to be a governess," I said. My mother uttered an exclamation of surprise, and laughed. My sister dropped her work in astonishment, exclaiming, "*You* a governess, Agnes! What can you be dreaming of?"

CHARLOTTE: (TO ANNE) I am amazed, Mr Bell. How can you dream so wantonly as to place yourself in the mind of a young girl? And, even more astonishing, one who wishes to be a governess! It is so far removed from your actual existence that I marvel at your powers of imagination!

EMILY: She must certainly suffer for her ambition. Do you not think so, Mr Bell? Read us now a passage where she suffers terribly! Read me the scene where she is tormented by that abominable snob Miss Murray.

ANNE: (THUMBING THROUGH BOOK) Wait, wait! Yes, I have it! (READS) "Miss Grey," said Miss Murray, as I was perusing a long and extremely interesting letter of my sister's, "Do put away that dull, stupid letter, and listen to me! You should tell the good people at home not to bore you with such long letters." (BEAT) "The good people at home," replied I, "know very well that the longer their letters are, the better I like them." (BEAT) "Well, said Miss Murray, "I want to talk about the ball; and to tell you that you positively must put off your holidays till it is over." (BEAT) "But," I said, "I cannot disappoint my friends by postponing my return so long. I cannot bear the thoughts of a Christmas spent from home."

EMILY: I like it. I like it that your Agnes should stand up for herself, stand up against the world. Stand up against the likes of Miss Murray.

CHARLOTTE: (SUDDENLY MELANCHOLY) Well, Christmas at home. That is a subtle victory and a mixed blessing perhaps. But it is something a governess will understand.

ANNE: (TO CHARLOTTE) Was not your own book about a governess?

CHARLOTTE: It was. And you will recall it was rejected by your publisher, despite the promise of payment from the author. Unlike your own works, which are now enjoying great celebrity...

EMILY: Nobody will read them. We have paid towards their publication and yet...

ANNE: We cannot pay the readers to read them. We had only one legacy from our poor aunt.

CHARLOTTE: But at least they are out in the world. At least they do not fester at home, as we do. At Christmas time or any other. (BEAT) Do you regret it then? Would you rather have spent the money on petticoats and bracelets?

ANNE: No, sister! I rejoice in being an authoress. And it is you who are the organiser of that.

CHARLOTTE: (TO ANNE) An *author*, Mr Bell. You are authors and you are men! (TO EMILY) And *you*, Mr Bell?

EMILY: To me it makes no difference. And yet... (BEAT) Perhaps it *was* good that we should do it. Even though I know not why.

ANNE: (TO CHARLOTTE) But you, Mr Bell, you are the one who provoked us to this action. It is unfair that you yourself should remain unpublished.

CHARLOTTE: The world is never fair. (BEAT) Come, let us drink the health of your publisher, gentlemen. God bless the man!

THEY DRINK A TOAST FROM THEIR FRUIT JUICE, THEN...

ANNE: Surely you have not surrendered your own literary hopes, Mr Bell?

CHARLOTTE: No, no, I am now working on a new tale. And I will seek out a new publisher. It is about a plain girl and I have called her Jane. I fear she is somewhat like myself.

EMILY: Is she a governess?

CHARLOTTE: I have not truly made up my mind on that score just yet.

EMILY: (JOSHING HER) She *will* be a governess, I know it!

ANNE: (TO CHARLOTTE) When you are published also, then we shall tell father. You will surely allow that?

EMILY: But how shall we ever tell Branwell? Tell me, Mr Bell. Tell me, Mr Organiser.

CHARLOTTE: If we are truly to be the Bells of the Ball, then we must learn to enjoy our secrets, smile behind our paper fans as we gaze at the dancing crowd. (BEAT)

72

Let us keep our own counsel on the matter. At least
for now. (BEAT) I am glad father has gone to bed.

SUDDEN BANGING AT THE DOOR. DRUNKEN
VOICES.

BRANWELL: (DISEMBODIED VOICE) Hey there! Let us
in!

BROWN: (DISEMBODIED VOICE) We demand
admission!

BRANWELL: (DISEMBODIED VOICE) Unless you be in a
state of undress!

BROWN: (DISEMBODIED VOICE) Even that I by no
means deplore!

SOUND OF DRUNKEN MALE LAUGHTER

EMILY: (SHOUTING) We are *not* in a state of
undress.

ANNE: Heaven forbid!

CHARLOTTE: Let them in then! (BEAT) But remember –
keep our own counsel.

EMILY GOES UPSTAGE LEFT, MIMES OPENING DOOR

EMILY: Come on in then! But do not wake our father!

BRANWELL AND JOHN BROWN ENTER. BRANWELL
IS LIGHTLY DRESSED IN WAISTCOAT AND
TROUSERS BUT JOHN BROWN WEARS THE
OVERCOAT AND TOP HAT THAT HE WORE IN THE
TAVERN. THEY STAGGER SLIGHTLY, WITH THEIR

FINGERS TO THEIR LIPS TO DENOTE A PLEDGE OF
SILENCE.

BRANWELL: Forgive us, ladies, for disturbing you!

CHARLOTTE: Why do men always believe they are
disturbing to women? And yet apologise for it?

BROWN: Thee is right, Miss Charlotte. There are too
many apologies in this world. Let us be simply as we
are, with no apologies. (BEAT) I for one pledge never
to apologise.

ANNE: But we are sinners, Mr Brown. And we must
sometimes apologise to God.

BRANWELL: I have brought John home with me...

EMILY: (STUDYING BROWN WITH INTEREST)
I can *see* you have brought Mr Brown home with you.

ANNE: Or *he* has brought *you* home.

CHARLOTTE: I can see you have been drinking. You have
both been drinking.

BROWN: (FORCEFULLY) No apologies, Miss
Charlotte.

JOHN BROWN WANDERS OVER TO THE TABLE, PUTS
HIS HAT ON IT, AND BEGINS TO PLAY IDLY WITH
THE SOLDIERS

BRANWELL: (IMITATING JOHN BROWN) No apologies,
sister.

BROWN: It has been a good night. Good for...

BRANWELL: Conversation.

BROWN: Argument.

BRANWELL: Philosophy.

BROWN: We have seen eternity tonight.

BRANWELL: Like a great ring of pure and endless light/ All calm as it was bright...

BROWN: Three hundred and sixty degrees as described by Euclid.

ANNE: I do not think our brother was talking mathematics, Mr Brown...

BROWN: (ARGUMENTATIVE) Was he not?

BRANWELL: (CONFUSED) Was I not?

BROWN: For what is philosophy except mathematics? What is the universe except an equation? A proof?

CHARLOTTE: A proof of what?

BROWN: Of itself.

ANNE: (IN SUPERIOR TONE) There we must differ, Mr Brown. To me and to my family, the universe is a manifestation of the love of God, a proof of that love.

BROWN: (INTENTLY TO ANNE) And what love has he shown to thee who has lost a mother and two sisters? (BEAT) Well, what is love? (TO THE COMPANY AS A WHOLE) As a tennis score it is nothing. Nowt. As nothing, we can multiply it and make it scores and hundreds and thousands and millions. Just by adding nowt and nowt and nowt.

ANNE: You are playing parlour games.

EMILY: But let him. Let him. I find it amusing.

BRANWELL: (STILL CONFUSED) Yes. Amusing...

BROWN: What is eternity then, if not mathematics? What is infinity? (BEAT) Well, I will tell thee: there is more than one infinity, as there is more than one God.

CHARLOTTE: That is blasphemy.

BROWN: Mere truth, Miss Charlotte. For tha must allow that there be an infinite number of numbers in the world. For numbers, like God, have no end.

CHARLOTTE: I do.

BROWN: But numbers are divided into odds and evens. And the number of even numbers is also infinite.

CHARLOTTE: Well...

BROWN: And for that matter, the number of odd numbers is infinite too.

EMILY: Ah, I see it.

BRANWELL: (ALWAYS A BEAT BEHIND) I too see it! Indeed I do!

BROWN: So we have already identified three separate infinities, have we not? And we have hardly begun. So many infinities!

BRANWELL: So many gods!

CHARLOTTE: (ANGRY NOW) Branwell!

BRANWELL: (APOLOGETIC) I do not mean...

BROWN: I think he was using metaphor, ma'am. I
            know from experience Mr Branwell is a master of
            metaphor. But it sometimes runs away with him.

EMILY: If there are many infinities, then there are
            many truths...

BROWN: Yes! Oh, tha's such a bright one, Miss Emily!
            (BEAT) All those truths! But not in the sense that
            parish records are a truth. What-does-tha-call-him was
            born on such-and-such and died on so-and-so. (PUTS
            HAND ON HEART) And I do attach to this
            document my signature that it is a true and accurate
            record. (BEAT) For when people die, then there is a
            need of parish record kind of truth. But epitaphs – are
            they also truths? *Gone to his Maker*? Do we know
            that for a parish record kind of truth? I think we do
            not. *Loved by all*? Show me a man who is loved by all
            and I'll eat a sod from the graveyard! No, no, not
            parish record truth at all! (BEAT) And all those
            poems. And all those novels...

EMILY: What truth are *they*, Mr Brown? For I have
            (BEAT) ambitions in that area.

BROWN: Does tha now, Miss Emily? (BEAT) Why, it
            is any truth tha could want! For a writer is like God, is
            he not? He makes a Universe on the page and
            sometimes we say: yes, it is true, it speaks to me of
            the world. But we know it is not the parish record
            kind of true. We know we cannot put our signatures to

it and say: this is an accurate record. (BEAT)
Suppose, for instance, in a century's time, some writer
might make a play out of all of us...

EMILY: (GIGGLES) Why should he do that?

BROWN: Who knows? *I* am not a writer. Perhaps he
has taken against us. Taken against *me*. He might
make me out the Devil Incarnate if he wanted. He
might write anything he liked. And it might not bear
one word of truth.

HE PICKS ONE UP ONE OF THE SOLDIERS

BROWN: Oh yes, he might treat us all like lead soldiers,
play with us, move us about, snap off our heads...

HE SNAPS OFF THE HEAD OF THE SOLDIER AND
THROWS IT ACROSS THE ROOM. CHARLOTTE AND
ANNE ARE CLEARLY SHOCKED BUT EMILY IS
AMUSED

EMILY: Was that not General Percy?

BRANWELL: (SHOCKED) We can perhaps repair him.

JOHN BROWN WALKS BACK TO WHERE EMILY
STANDS. THEY STARE INTENTLY AT EACH OTHER
FOR A MINUTE, THEN...

BROWN: But thee, Miss Emily... (PASSIONATELY)
Oh yes, I should like to read a novel written by thee. I
should not be surprised if thee did not turn out the
brightest star in the vault!

HE STARES AT HER UNTIL SHE LOOKS AWAY,
EMBARRASSED BUT PLEASED. HE THEN TURNS AND
ADDRESSES THE COMPANY AS A WHOLE

BROWN: That is to say, the vault of heaven of course.
Though I am a gravedigger, yet I did not mean
anything so unfeeling as the *family* vault. No offence
intended!

BRANWELL: None taken!

EMILY: None at all!

CHARLOTTE: So numbers govern everything, Mr Brown?
Not love, nor decency, nor sense of duty? Only
numbers.

BROWN: Does not the Bible itself tell us this, Miss
Charlotte? For I saw a new heaven and a new earth!
And at the Gates twelve angels! And on the gates the
names of the twelve tribes of Israel! And the wall of
the city had twelve foundations and on them the
twelve names of the twelve apostles! And are there
not twelve pence in a shilling? And will that state not
continue evermore till the very crack of doom?

BRANWELL: (STUNNED) It must be so!

BROWN: (TO THE COMPANY) And are we not all
here, ladies, to make up the ledger as the Great
Accountant demands? And is that not enough?

HE TURNS TO EMILY AGAIN

BROWN: It is a shame, Miss Emily, that there is no
music in this house tonight, for Mr Branwell and I
have been discussing music.

EMILY: And if there *were*, Mr Brown, what should we
        do?

BROWN: Why then, we should dance!

EMILY: It would wake father!

BROWN: Not if we dance without music. We can easily
        do so. All we need are the measures!

HE STARES INTO HER EYES. SHE RETURNS THE
GAZE AND, IN A FLIRTATIOUS GESTURE, UNWINDS
THE HEAD SCARF AND THROWS IT DOWN. HE
TAKES HER IN HIS ARMS AND BEGINS A CLUMSY
WALTZ ROUND THE ROOM

BROWN: One-two-three, one-two-three, one-two-three!
        One-two-three, one-two-three, one-two-three! One-
        two-three, one-two-three, one-two-three!

AS THEY COMPLETE A CIRCLE OF THE STAGE,
EMILY SUDDENLY BREAKS DOWN IN GIGGLES AND
PULLS AWAY FROM HIM

EMILY: It is too strange, Mr Brown!

BROWN: Strange? No, there is no strangeness. (BEAT)
        We are all of a muchness, are we not? All of a mean
        and an average? So why do we strive, to be other than
        we are? Are we not already sufficient?

BRANWELL: Yes. It is so!

CHARLOTTE LEAPS ANGRILY TO HER FEET

CHARLOTTE: (SHOUTING) No, Mr Brown! No, brother!
        We are not in this world to make up the numbers! We

are here to show our Maker who and what we are!
Yes, Mr Brown, we are here to strive!

BRANWELL: (TRYING TO INTERRUPT) But sister...

CHARLOTTE: (VERY ANGRY NOW) Hush, Branwell! We
have heard enough of you!

SHE TURNS TO ADDRESS EMILY

CHARLOTTE: And you, sister! I condemn you for your
slatternly behaviour!

EMILY: I do not understand...

CHARLOTTE: Look at this room! Is this what passes for
neatness in your outlandish world? Is it tidy? Is it
right? Is it fit for a Christian family? Must we not
labour far more diligently to clear away the bric-a-
brac?

SHE PICKS UP THE BROOM FROM THE SIDE OF THE
DESK AND ADVANCES ON JOHN BROWN

CHARLOTTE: You dance, Mr Brown? You enjoy the dance?
You admire the terpsichorean art?

BROWN: (TAKEN ABACK) Why, yes, Miss...

CHARLOTTE BEGINS TO SWEEP HIM AWAY,
KNOCKING THE BROOM AGAINST HIS ANKLES,
FORCING HIM TO DANCE ACROSS THE ROOM. LIKE
EMILY AND JOHN BROWN PREVIOUSLY, THEY
MAKE A COMPLETE CIRCLE OF THE STAGE

BROWN: (SHOCKED AND PROTESTING) Miss
        Charlotte! (LOOKING PLEADINGLY AT EMILY)
        Miss Emily!

EMILY COLLAPSES IN LAUGHTER. ANNE JOINS IN.
CHARLOTTE STOPS THE ATTACK AND CATCHES
HER BREATH

CHARLOTTE: Yes, we are here to strive, Mr Brown.
        (MORE CALMLY) And now I would be happy if you
        were to strive to leave this house.

BROWN: (VERY SUBSERVIENT ALL OF A
        SUDDEN) If that is thy wish, ma'am. If that is the
        wish of the other ladies. If that is the wish of Miss
        Emily..

HE WALKS ACROSS TO THE TABLE AND PICKS UP
HIS HAT, THEN MOVES ACROSS TO EMILY. THEY
STARE AT EACH OTHER FOR A MOMENT.
EVENTUALLY SHE DROPS HER EYES

BROWN: Oh, for thee, bright Emily, for thee I would...

EMILY: (LOOKING HIM IN THE EYES AGAIN)
        What would you do?

BROWN: Why, I would hang a litter of puppies!

HE TURNS ON HIS HEEL AND EXITS UPSTAGE LEFT,
BRISKLY AND WITH NO SIGN OF DRUNKENNESS

BRANWELL: (HE TURNS ON CHARLOTTE) You have
        insulted my friend!

CHARLOTTE IGNORES HIM

CHARLOTTE: (TO THE GIRLS) Come. It is late and there
   will be even more jollification in the morning. We
   must be ready for the high spirits of the day.

THE GIRLS TROOP OUT SLOWLY UPSTAGE RIGHT.
CHARLOTTE TAKES EMILY'S ARM

CHARLOTTE: Plain Jane. She *will* be a governess. I know
   her well. I am *good* at governesses.

THEY EXIT UPSTAGE RIGHT. BRANWELL
CONTINUES TO STAND AS IF STUNNED. AFTER A
MINUTE HE MAKES HIS WAY ACROSS TO THE DESK,
PICKS UP HIS DRESSING GOWN FROM THE CHAIR,
PUTS IT ON, SITS AT THE DESK AND GAZES INTO
THE MIDDLE DISTANCE, THEN...

BRANWELL: (VIOLENTLY PULLING PAPERS OUT OF
   THE DRAWERS AND READING FROM THEM IN
   AN AGITATED MANNER, THROWING THEM
   DOWN AS HE DOES SO) The Editor of
   Blackwoods. Sir, Read what I write. It is right that
   you must. I trust you will not think me used and stale
   that I have already been published in the Halifax
   Guardian. (LAUGHS) The Secretary, The Royal
   Academy. Sir, We had arranged an appointment but
   there was family business. That is plain truth. I swear
   it. My family inquired of Mr Turner and Mr
   Gainsborough. But these true artists would simply not
   permit me to call on you. (LAUGHS) The Directors
   of the Leeds and Manchester Railroad. I write to bring
   to your attention a very grave injustice that I will take
   to my grave. Yes, you see now how I am so very
   talented at wordplay! (BEAT) A sum of money has
   been lost. Lost. Yes. Lost forever. (BEAT) I will
   make no halt. I will be received by the Lady of the

Mansion in the breakfast room. Breakfast is so intimate. (BEAT) I recall the promise lately given to my father. Where is the artillery? I was promised artillery. No mind. The battle is lost. Forever. (BEAT) Leyland, teacher of my art, there is a lady about whom I had such high hopes. I wait each day, breathless. But I am surrounded by powerful persons who hate me. And she is lost. (BEAT) Lydia, teacher of my heart, I had such high hopes of you. I wait and wait. But you are lost. (BEAT) I never hoped for your husband's death. Never. I swear. I never hoped for him to be lost. I hope only for honour and respect for every degree, kind and appetite... (BEAT) Powerful persons... Watching me. (HE LOOKS ROUND SUSPICIOUSLY) Though they hate me, they will not tear from my heart the thousand recollections. They will not take from me the sunlight. (VOICE RISES) Do not let me be lost, O Great Editor. Do not let me be lost, father! (BEAT) Also, I had written a poem, and a novel which I have now lost. Lost. Forever lost.(SEARCHES DRAWERS) Where, where..? I can find nothing! I therefore wait each day, breathless. (VOICE RISES) I have been waiting so long, father! So very long!

HE LEAPS TO HIS FEET, RUNS ACROSS THE ROOM, TEARING UP THE PAPERS, THROWING THEM WILDLY AROUND HIM. HE CIRCLES THE STAGE, BANGS HIS FISTS ON THE DESK, ONE-TWO-THREE, ONE-TWO-THREE, ONE-TWO-THREE, ONE-TWO-THREE, HOLDS HIS HEAD AND BEGINS TO CRY. FINALLY HE FALLS BACK IN THE CHAIR AND SLUMPS HEAD FIRST ON THE DESK. THE LIGHTS GO OUT SUDDENLY. SILENCE

ACT II, SCENE 5.

AFTER A MINUTE A SPOTLIGHT FALLS ON
BRANWELL

ENTER CHARLOTTE UPSTAGE RIGHT. SHE WALKS
INTO THE SPOTLIGHT, PUTS A HAND ON HER
BROTHER'S SHOULDER AND SHAKES HIM

CHARLOTTE: Brother! Brother! Be awake!

THERE IS NO RESPONSE FROM BRANWELL

CHARLOTTE: (HER VOICE RAISED NOW) Brother!
    Brother! Be awake!

AGAIN SHE SHAKES HIM, AGAIN THERE IS NO
RESPONSE. SHE PUTS HER HANDS TO HER HEAD
AND...

THERE IS THE LOUD, HIGH, PIERCING SCREAM OF A
WOMAN. SPOT GOES OUT. ALL IS DARKNESS

ACT II, SCENE 6.

WE HEAR THE HYMN *O GOD OUR HELP IN AGES PAST*
AS SUNG BY A CHURCH CONGREGATION

CONGREGATION: (DISEMBODIED VOICES) O God,
    our help in ages past, Our hope for years to come,/Our
    shelter from the stormy blast, And our eternal home./
    Under the shadow of Thy throne Still may we dwell
    secure;/ Sufficient is Thine arm alone, And our
    defence is sure./ Before the hills in order stood, Or

earth received her frame,/ From everlasting Thou art God, To endless years the same./

AS HYMN FADES, WE HEAR BIRDSONG. SPOTLIGHT FOLLOWS PATRICK WHO ENTERS DOWNSTAGE RIGHT, CARRYING A BIBLE. HE WALKS SLOWLY CENTRE STAGE AND ADDRESSES THE AUDIENCE

PATRICK: In the midst of life...

HE CHOKES A LITTLE THEN CONTINUES...

PATRICK: We are here to mourn but also to celebrate. We celebrate a life of talent and richness. We celebrate a life lived fully and in God's grace. (HE OPENS THE BIBLE) The lesson for today is from Job, Chapter 1, verse 21: *Naked came I out of my mother's womb and naked shall I return thither...*

A SECOND SPOT SUDDENLY LIGHTS UP JOHN BROWN DOWNSTAGE LEFT. HE CARRIES HIS SHOVEL. HE TOO ADDRESSES THE AUDIENCE

BROWN: Mourn. Celebrate. Talent. Richness. Grace. Lesson. (BEAT) What do words mean? They mean anything. They mean nothing.

PATRICK: (STILL ADDRESSING AUDIENCE, APPARENTLY UNAWARE OF JOHN BROWN) The Lord gave and the Lord hath taken away...

BROWN: (STILL ADDRESSING AUDIENCE) Give and take away! Addition and subtraction! The sums go on forever! (HE LAUGHS)

PATRICK: (ADDRESSING AUDIENCE, STILL APPARENTLY UNAWARE OF JOHN BROWN)

Blessed be the name of the Lord. (HE CLOSES THE BIBLE) My daughter Charlotte was the final child of mine to die. Not one of them was spared to his allotted span. Yet Charlotte has given the world her words...

BROWN: (STILL ADDRESSING AUDIENCE) Writers! Poets! What do they know? They fret and posture and pretend they give us meaning. But they give us only their madness...

PATRICK: (TURNS TO JOHN BROWN) Do your work, Brown. I must speak with Mrs Gaskell before she leaves. She is even now preparing an account of Charlotte's life and the lives of her brother and sisters. So those lives will not be unknown, will not be in vain. For that we must be grateful.

BROWN: (STILL ADDRESSING AUDIENCE) Grateful? Nay, I am not grateful. I shall take comfort only in inches, ounces, gallons, the stuff of measuring. Because it is they give the only truth to this life, those things that yield measurement.

JOHN BROWN BEGINS SHOVELLING, THEN STOPS

BROWN: (GLANCING AT PATRICK) It has been hard for thee, parson. All thy chickens dead. But what were they in the end but quantities, volumes, lengths, weights and capacities? A Branwell or a Charlotte? What is the difference? And are the rest of us not the same? (HE DROPS HIS SPADE) Tha's lost thy children. I will be thy child. Tha's lost a son. I will be thy son. Tha's lost a wife. I will be thy wife. (HE OPENS HIS ARMS TO EMBRACE PATRICK)

PATRICK: (IGNORING THIS) I will leave you now. I must converse with the mourners, with those who loved her.

EXIT PATRICK SLOWLY DOWNSTAGE RIGHT. JOHN BROWN WATCHES HIM GO THEN MOVES CENTRE STAGE

BROWN: (ADDRESSING AUDIENCE AGAIN) For what is that final number, that infinity of all the infinities? It is six foot by six foot by two. I tell you this: every day I dig and every day I spend my hours measuring the world. (BEAT) And what is poetry? Only measures and metre. And what is music? Only numbers. (HE HOLDS OUT HIS ARMS LIKE A MAN TAKING A DANCE PARTNER, THEN WALTZES ACROSS THE STAGE, FOLLOWED BY THE SPOT) One two three, Miss Emily, one two three, one two three! One two three, one two three, one two three. (HE COMPLETES A COMPLETE CIRCLE OF THE STAGE THEN STOPS, FACES AUDIENCE AGAIN) She should have danced! She should have danced with *me*! She should *not* have refused!

HE STANDS STOCK-STILL AND REPEATEDLY CLENCHES AND UNCLENCHES HIS FISTS. THEN HE STARTS TO DANCE AGAIN, ROUND AND ROUND, ROUND AND ROUND...

BROWN: One two three! One two three! One two three! One two three!

HE FREEZES. WE HEAR THE DIES IRAE FROM
MOZART'S REQUIEM. AFTER A MINUTE, THE LIGHTS
DIM. THE MUSIC FADES.

ALL IS DARKNESS AND SILENCE

THE END

About the author

Michael Yates was successively reporter and film critic on the *Sheffield Star* newspaper, and also worked as a subeditor for the *Bradford Telegraph & Argus* and the *Huddersfield Examiner.*

He taught playwriting at Harrogate Theatre and creative writing for the Workers Educational Association, and in 2010 was Writer in Residence in Bradford Schools.

He has had short stories published in magazines and anthologies and won short story prizes from the Jersey Arts Centre, The Armagh Writers Festival, the Wolds Words Festival and the Writers & Artists Yearbook. Michael has been Poet in Residence in Whitby, in Wakefield Hospitals and at Wakefield Cathedral and has published three volumes of verse.

A dozen of Michael's plays have been performed in the North of England, including Manchester, Liverpool, Leeds, Bradford and Wakefield; and one of his plays won the Stanley Arnold Trophy at the Sheffield One-Act Play Festival.

Also by Michael Yates in Nettle Books

Life Class

A collection of more than 90 poems about life, love and plenty of other things that don't even alliterate! *"Delight in the careful observations and appreciate the wisdom of the depictions, for reading this book is truly a life class"* – John Irving Clarke in his introduction.

£9.95.   ISBN 978-0-9561513-0-8

#0093 - 251017 - C0 - 210/148/5 - PB - DID2001889